AMNESIA

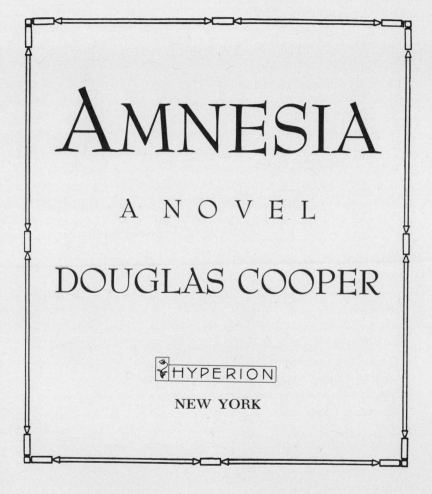

AMNESIA

A NOVEL

DOUGLAS COOPER

HYPERION

NEW YORK

Library of Congress Cataloging-in-Publication Data

Cooper, Douglas.
    Amnesia : a novel / Douglas Cooper. — 1st ed.
      p.   cm.
    ISBN 1-56282-748-0
    1. Psychological fiction.   I. Title.
    PR9199.3.C6435A8   1994
    813′.54—dc20   93-27929
                                                                      CIP

Designed by Gloria Adelson

First American Edition

10 9 8 7 6 5 4 3 2 1

For Laura

Acknowledgments

To my editors, Doug Pepper and Mary Ann Naples.

To my agents, Rod Hall and Ellen Levine.

To the late Frances Yates, whose research into the history of mnemonics I have cheerfully distorted.

To all those who read drafts.

To the Canada Council, for the generous award of an Explorations Grant.

To Atom and Eve.

To Garret and Alex, for feeding me in Paris.

To the late Ficciones Bookstore in Montreal.

To my family.

To my dear friend, Ruth Abbey.

CONTENTS

AMNESIA

1

ARCHIVE

A young girl like you lives all her life beside a lake; she loves the lake like a seagull, and, like a seagull, is happy and free. A man comes along by chance, sees her, and having nothing better to do, destroys her, just like this seagull here.

Trigorin, The Seagull

THERE IS NO CURE IN TALKING. Izzy insisted upon this, and yet he came to me, confessing everything: his own crime, his monstrous nature, and other crimes, crimes that he had only witnessed, the acts of men who made him seem almost innocent by comparison.

He is a monster of sorts. By his own admission, he does not deserve to be forgiven. I understand that his story might well be dangerous with lies; even so I would have to agree, if only for what he has done to me in the short time I have known him.

His name is not short for Isaac, Isaiah, or Israel, though

he has been called all of these, and more. He was born "Izzy." In proof, he showed me his birth certificate, which I stared at with some interest since I do not have one. The plastic cover is growing yellow with age and has tinted the blue certificate green. Izzy Darlow.

"There is no cure in talking if we are essentially alone."

Izzy came into my office four hours before I was to be married. I was not working. I was there because it made sense to me to spend the morning in my office on that day, after which my life would never again be the same. I would calm myself in advance by sitting in a familiar room, one of the few rooms I knew well.

The fall was just beginning then; now it is almost winter. Izzy's entrance into my office was camouflaged by the rattle of the window in its frame. The caulking has rotted; the glass is so old that it refracts the view; and the frame, probably loose to begin with, has expanded with water and bent. As a result, I feel the seasons as strongly indoors as I do on the street. I hear them as well.

Fall is a terrible noise. The winds are pulled out of shape by the bank towers and no longer know whether they are coming or going. Every change in the wind brings a change in the rain and a change in the rhythm of the glass.

This change, however, this latest movement of the fall air, brought a man, perhaps twenty-three, shivering and nerve-shot, to the foot of my desk. I looked up, and he was there.

The man wore a frayed vest, the last remaining piece

of a three-piece suit. It was a herringbone pattern; the silk in back had been worn to a shine. He wore a shirt that might once have been formal, but it had not been ironed in years and the collar curled like a dead leaf against his neck. His trousers, striped gray and white, had once perhaps formed the bottom half of a morning suit. I sensed these were the only clothes he owned. Maybe, like his clothes, he had once been presentable, almost appealing, but that time was past.

"You work with plans, don't you?"

I am an archival librarian, and yes, I work with plans. Without waiting for an answer, he leaned forward and read the quotation I have framed on my desk.

"Do you like Freud?"

"I like that quotation. Excuse me, I'm not working today. If there's anything I can do for you quickly . . ."

"No, not quickly."

"Then perhaps you can come back on Monday, and one of the librarians . . ."

He sat down. "Why do you like Freud?"

"I said I like the quotation. I like what it expresses. It struck me as appropriate, since I work with plans of the city—"

"I think you can help me."

"Look, I'm sorry. If you come back Monday—"

"Do you have some time?"

"I'm going to be married in less than four hours!"

"Ah. What are you doing till then?"

He had me. I was doing nothing. I was expressly doing nothing. My fiancée's father, who was paying for everything, was taking great pride in the preparations, and he wanted me elsewhere. I considered lying, but I do not lie easily.

"Nothing," I said. I leaned back and sighed. "What can I do for you?"

I like your quotation, because it has little to do with Freud. He borrowed the idea. He in fact rejects the idea a few pages later. The idea, however—the analogy—is important. It is the clue to everything.

The mind is like a city.

Izzy sat facing me, in a chair that was the mirror image of mine. The desk was a perfect rectangle. I had moved the desk into the very center of the room, so that I could roll out a plan on the surface and gather a conference around it. If you sliced the room horizontally through the window and photographed it from above, you would need subtle clues to discern north from south. The window was the same width as the door. The moldings were of the same wood. My hair, however, was parted on the left and Izzy's on the right. Viewed in plan, the room was symmetrical about the axis that divided the desk between us.

"The mind is like a city. If you can remember this, then you can remember all things. Freud, who in time forgot everything important, soon forgot this as well. He briefly compared the mind to the Eternal City, then dismissed the analogy as absurd. And when he had forgotten everything important, he was ready to found the science of modern depth psychology. I cannot tell

6

you how much my friends have suffered because of that man."

I found Izzy's views on Freud arrogant. I would not presume to dismiss a man of Freud's stature. There was something visceral about this hatred, however; it was not so much an intellectual stance as a personal grudge, and this compensated for his tone.

"Katie . . . poor Katie, I wonder if she is still alive. She was ruined by that man."

"I'm sorry," I said in irritation, "I don't know who this person is."

"Wait," said Izzy. "You will know her."

My story is old. When it was told by Shakespeare, it was called a tragedy. Chekhov called his a comedy, though it is hard to say why *The Seagull* is any less painful than *Hamlet*. This very old story has found its way into my life, and it is too early to decide what I shall call it. It all depends upon Katie.

Something about this story makes it want to replicate, breed inwardly like cancer. Plays within plays, stories within stories. The smallest part of this tale contains within it, like a hologram, the beginning, middle, and end.

I will tell you, now, what this story is going to be. I will tell you again, and again. Yet you will forget. I know you will. I did. You will forget, and feel every event in your reader's eyes as if it were being encountered for the first time. "No recollection," says Trigorin, musing. "No recollection. . . ."

* * *

I am Jewish, said Izzy. This means that I am required to take a strong stance concerning memory. The Orthodox have a saying: "May his name and memory be erased." The modern Jews say something else: "We shall never forget." How you stand in regard to these sayings will determine who you are.

As he said this, he stared at me with meaning. Does he know something, I wondered. I do not think I am Jewish. I am quite sure I am not Jewish. But I have had my troubles with memory.

"I will tell you about Katie," he said. "She told me her story, and I will tell it to you. It is a dangerous story. It is the kind of story that finds its way into your life, like a spore, and grows. Katie's story grew in my own life until it was so intricately entwined in my own story that I could no longer separate. That may happen to you."

I laughed. But that was the first week of fall, and now it is almost winter. Katie's story has wound itself about me so completely that my fiancée has become a mere detail in its telling. As I listened to Izzy Darlow confess, my own wedding became a small fact, and then a possibility, and then, over the course of those hours, it dwindled in importance until I knew that I would never be married.

Katie lived in a large house built into the side of the ravine. The driveway plunged over the lip of the cliff with such urgency that most of her parents' friends were afraid to descend in their cars. They would park on the street. When her father drove down to the garage, he would press the brake pedal to the floor, and even then it seemed as if the car would never stop in time, as if it would ring against the garage door like a hammer, bend it from its sockets, and shatter the back wall into shards of concrete, as if her family would career out and over the ravine, perching in the air for a moment before igniting the landscape below with their explosive demise. But this never happened.

Somehow, Katie's father would always bring the car to a safe halt some feet in front of the door. Perhaps this was why she emerged from childhood with the sense that she was charmed and probably invulnerable. I had never had this sense, and it left me in awe.

Katie would run from the car to the garage and pull with all her might at the handle of the steel door. It would rise like a miracle and roll up into the ceiling of the garage, though it weighed perhaps five times as much as she did. For years she had the sense that she could lift anything, because the world, no matter how heavy it looked, was light.

"When Katie first told me this," said Izzy, "she was wearing an ill-fitting hospital gown that kept falling open at the back. Despite her change in fortune, it was easy to believe her. Even later, when she had been completely ruined, she had a way of carrying herself so that you knew she had not been born into slavery."

Her bedroom was cantilevered out over the ravine. Three of the four walls had been pierced by windows so she could look out into the land far below, far enough below that the wolves who bred with dogs could not reach her. They could see her, though, staring out on moonlit nights, and they would jump ferociously, making the sounds of lust.

"Our dog," said Izzy, "was part wolf."

"Our dog had been rescued from the thieves in the ravine, who had starved it and made it murderous. My brother Aaron had found it, so weak that its efforts to kill him were pathetic and almost endearing." Aaron had been sleeping in the shadows at the foot of the ravine—a foolish thing to do, but he was fearless—when this skeletal dog had woken him, its teeth about his throat. But it was too weak to close its jaw and had just lain there, on the verge of killing him, whimpering. Aaron had taken it home.

"It is well known that huskies have wolf in them. Our dog, who had been conceived in the ravine that yawned beneath Katie's house, had more than most."

The ravine was a place where the city combined with the darkness, a place of confrontation. It was part of a network of wild spaces that laced the body of the city like a net of veins. Men would throw bridges over the ravine, effortless bridges; they would walk the air between the edges of the ravine and tell themselves that they had tamed it.

Few had the courage to build a house where Katie's father had built his.

The permutations available to the mind in the full daylight of the commercial city are restricted by convention. Houses can be shaped only a certain number of ways; buildings are mute and graceless; men and women self-effacing. In the ravine, this rule cannot be enforced.

The dominant rule in the city is propriety, and it is enforced by shame. Shame, however, is a function of daylight. In the ravine, where the shadows shift and move like thieves, there are no witnesses.

Shame is a function of sight. When a citizen of the streets walks through the ravine, unwatched, he can choose to take his propriety with him. He can police himself. He might choose to do this: to carry his shame with him, in the form of guilt. Then again, he might not.

The permutations available to the mind in the ravine are infinite. Dogs breed with wolves. There is nothing to prevent, for instance, the birth of a beast. A new combination. The head of a man, say, and the monstrous thighs of a lion. It is not inconceivable.

The entire city is mapped in the Archive. We can trace the horizontal evolution of every building and street in Toronto. In a sense, the Archive is very much like Rome in Freud's analogy to the mind: an impossible city in which everything exists simultaneously. A building that was torn down a hundred years ago coexists with the present building, occupying the same site. Nothing is ever destroyed. Everything is remembered.

The ravines, however, mock our rational efforts. They are the margins on the edge of the known; not so much the forgotten as the unlearned. The ancient mapmakers would label their despair with the words "Here Be Dragons." We label ours with something more banal, hoping to render it innocuous.

"Evil," said Izzy, "resides in the white spaces between consciousness."

Together we took out the most recent map of the ravine. It was really a map of the bridges and spaces over and beside the ravine, because the ravine itself is uncharted. We located Katie's house. The house was cross-referenced to a set of documents relating to its construction. We took these out as well.

There had been some problem convincing the planners that a house should be built there, in the wall of the ravine. It did not specifically contravene zoning laws, but it was considered vaguely obscene, improper; the censors were consulted for their views, even though they of course had no jurisdiction over such things.

The censors, in fact, were instrumental in clearing the application. The house, they said, could easily be classified as artistic, since it was willfully inaccessible and perverse. When a film was deemed artistic, the censors made a generous effort to be lenient. They suggested that the city planners might wish to follow their example.

It wasn't so much that the censors approved of art. It was a practical matter. If something were inaccessible—say, an experimental film—it would marginalize itself. It would not command a large audience. Decent citizens would be rightly ashamed to come in contact with it. Hence it engaged in a form of self-censorship, which was almost acceptable (and eminently Torontonian).

The house had been built.

As a girl, Katie hardly slept at all when the moon was full. She kept a vigil at her window, staring out between the shifting trees. The moonlight was never strong enough to illuminate much, but sometimes she felt certain that she could see something, some incomprehensible activity at the edge of the shadows.

She composed stories, which she would tell to the chief doll in her collection, the twisted one that she adored because she could tell it anything. Most of the dolls her mother had purchased in fashionable stores on Cumberland or Bloor. They had shiny faces and perfect features, and seemed to mock Katie's spindly body, which was pointy and had scabs and its own intensity of posture. She had never found this in any doll.

One of the cats from the ravine had taken to leaving dead birds on the doorstep. Katie buried these in the back garden, with compassion and some interest, and for her efforts was rewarded: after months of tiny corpses, the cat dragged in an ancient doll out of the brush, rotten and half-chewed. Katie took it upstairs with her, and it became her audience.

Her mother continued to buy her good dolls, which Katie would put in the closet for safekeeping. Three times she had to rescue the twisted doll from the garbage, before her mother relinquished all hopes of doing away with it. Katie was quietly willful.

When the moonlight yielded something particularly ambiguous and thought-provoking, Katie would work it into a long story, which she would tell to the crippled doll on her bed. Together they investigated the meaning of the ravine.

Aaron carried the dog home, so that our youngest brother, Josh, could give it a name.

13

"It'th kind of unhealthy," said Josh, disturbed.

Josh had a speech impediment, which somehow never prevented him from becoming the most eloquent among us. He was two years younger than me, five years younger than Aaron, but he had a depth and calmness of spirit that made him the favorite. My older brother and I were bound up in pettiness and hatred from the moment we could speak, but Josh seemed capable of moving through the confusion of private life without resentment.

"It'th thtarving . . ."

Josh did not like furniture, and would curl in corners like a monkey. He was also happy on the stairs, which is where he now sat. He had the eyes of a nocturnal animal, wide and much too large. They were blue, whereas the rest of us had black Semitic eyes, mostly pupil. His hair was fine and almost red.

Aaron, cradling the dog, had a shock of dark hair, which would have hidden his eyes had they not been even darker. My impression of Aaron is that his face was always in shadow.

I examined Izzy as he described his brothers. He certainly seemed to take after Aaron more than he did Josh. His hair was straight, but tangled and almost black. It was parted without skill, showing a jagged line of scalp. His eyebrows were prominent. They looked themselves as if they could use combing. They cast deep shadows about his eyes.

"You have to feed it thomething."

"Yeah, I know. Look, why don't you give it a name. I'm going to keep it."

"Ith it a boy or girl?"

Aaron looked. "Female."

"I'll thee what I can do . . ."

Josh curled his arms about his knees and huddled his head down, as he did when he was thinking. I had been watching this conversation from the alcove beside the stairs, and I thought I might contribute to the naming.

"Why don't you call it—"

"Who the fuck asked you."

"Well, it's going to be a family pet if you keep it—"

"It's going to be *my* pet. I found it; I'm gonna name it; I'm gonna keep it."

Josh lifted his head, his huge eyes bright. "Thapphire."

Aaron stared at the dog, whose coat was a jaundiced gray, and lifted an eyebrow dubiously. "Sapphires are blue."

"It'th a good name. Thapphire. That'th what you should call it."

Aaron pondered this. Joshua usually had his reasons. "Okay. Sapphire."

Aaron put his mouth close to the dog's ear. "Hey, Sapphire . . ."

The dog rolled her starved head in Aaron's arms, and whined.

The dog became a family pet, despite Aaron's constant insistence that she belonged exclusively to him. We took turns feeding her: at first liquids and then various soft foods, until she was healthy again.

Sapphire never lost her murderous qualities. She kept

15

the other children in the neighborhood in constant terror, and a legend grew up and around her, enumerating babies she had stolen from the cradle and eaten without remorse. She was always good to us, however, because we had saved her from starvation. I'm sure, as well, that she was treated much better by us than she had been by the thieves in the ravine.

When she was again fully healthy, Sapphire's coat took on a distinctly blue cast.

An hour had passed, and Izzy showed no sign of drawing his story to a close. It did not, in fact, seem yet to be a single story.

"What did Katie have to do with Aaron?"

"Nothing. They never met. I didn't meet Katie myself until many years later, and by then I had little to do with Aaron."

"So you're telling me two stories . . ."

"Many."

"I have to be married in three hours."

"But they wind together, pull apart . . . you know . . ."

"I have three hours!"

Izzy smiled, and dropped his eyes, as if he knew something.

It was not the first time I had had the sense that he was one step ahead of me. Then again, it was hard for me because of my circumstances. If I were to worry that everybody I met had secret knowledge of my life before the trauma, I would go mad with suspicion.

I have tried to live in naive trust. I assume the best of people, and am often rewarded with precisely that.

Nevertheless, it was difficult not to read meaning into Izzy's smile: he knew something, something important about me. He had a sense that I had misgivings about the woman I was soon to marry.

"By the time I met Katie," he resumed, "we had both changed. Not simply grown, but changed. Encountered something. Never recovered."

Despite her proximity to the ravine, Katie was unqualified in her hospitality. Half-eaten dolls, dead birds—nothing in her world was unredeemable, and everything was, to a degree, interesting. Hence, everything was welcome.

She welcomed the change in the seasons, though summer would leave her with a heat rash that turned her red and made sleep impossible. She enjoyed the fall, despite the cold that would take her with the first rain and not depart until the leaves were gone. She was too thin to spend much time out of doors in winter before her extremities froze painfully. Spring was the only innocuous time of year, and she welcomed it as well.

During the spring she would leave at least two of the windows open. This sent an intermittent draft across her bed and helped her to sleep. She would lie on top of the covers in an old cotton shift and wait for the air to move. Sometimes the current of air created a momentary vacuum, and she would wake up, breathless, as the door pulled shut with a bang. For some people these are moments of terror, the waking into death, but Katie would smile and close her eyes again. Within moments she would be asleep.

That was why she was not frightened by the first visitor.

The air was close, for spring, and though she had all three windows open, she could not sleep. She could smell the green awakening in the trees, and the water rising invisibly from the soil. On nights like this she would sit cross-legged on her pillow and tell a story to the doll, the twisted one, who sat facing her at the foot of the bed.

"There was a girl," said Katie. "She was alone, but she wasn't alone. You know, she was okay, it was all right. So this girl . . . Actually, she wasn't really a girl. She was a bird.

"There was a bird," said Katie. "Are you listening?"

The doll was. Katie clasped her hands together, satisfied.

"She flew a lot. When she wasn't flying, she ate bugs. Sometimes she flew and ate bugs all at the same time. Right?"

The twisted one agreed. This is what the bird did.

"Good. She had her own lake."

Katie stopped and thought on this, briefly thrilled. That would be a good thing, to have your own lake.

"This girl—I mean, this bird—really liked the lake. She was a lake bird."

A lake bird, thought Katie. Not quite right. And then: "She was a seagull!"

She frowned, and thought hard on this. "No," she said. "No, a lake gull."

This brought a satisfied smile to her face, and the twisted one smiled with her, though it had lost a great piece of smile in the ravine.

"This lake gull was eating bugs one day. She was actually flying and eating bugs, all at the same time. She was happy. She'd just got a bug, and was eating it, when she saw the man."

Katie was lost for a moment, because now it was necessary to think the man, to decide who he was and what he was doing by the lake, which belonged to the gull and not to him; she was lost and glanced at the window for guidance.

It was perched there, chewing with noise on a large dragonfly.

Izzy had become pale. This part of the story proved difficult. His hands, which had been shaking from the start, gripped the plan in front of him, as if he hoped that holding on to something fragile might steady his fingers. Yet they still shook, and in fact convulsed once, so that he inadvertently tore a piece of vellum from the corner of the drawing.

"Sorry," he said, mortified. It was clear he had some respect for archival material—I noted this, and he nodded.

"Libraries . . . ," he said. "Libraries are important."

I was hounded into the library from the first day of grade one. Aaron had been at school before me and had prepared them for my arrival. They were on his side; everybody was always on Aaron's side; he had won them over. I was six years old. I knew they were going to eat me alive, so I hid in the library before and after school.

I could already read and write. My parents made sure we could before we went to school. It was soon clear that grade one would be a waste of time, so my teacher let me spend entire days in the library. I suppose I looked pitiful, hiding up there, but I was determined to find a world in books. The world outside was too dangerous.

I was wrong, of course. About the relative danger of the world outside. There was a world on the shelf of the library—a world on the second shelf from the floor, though I did not discover it until some time later—a world far more appalling than anything I would encounter in the violence of the family.

Izzy sat alone at the small table in the corner of the library for some time before he was noticed. He was small for his age and rarely stood out. He had become an expert at blending in with his environment, because the less he attracted attention at home, the less he was the subject of abuse. Aaron merely had to see him to start. So he had become a chameleon.

For days he sat there, while other students did time around him. Few people went to the library unless sentenced. He found a book on the internal combustion engine and stared at the pictures. None of his toys had prepared him for the secret life of the engine. It had cycles of hunger, inspiration, and explosion; it was voracious and relentless and unspeakably modern. One day, while staring at this book, he began to cry.

A man with silver hair sat down beside him. His thin shoulders pushed up to the sides of his neck as he sat down; they pointed towards the ceiling like the folded wings of a bat. He came and sat there, and for a moment said nothing, not even staring at Izzy, who cried into the book.

Without turning, the man said, "That must be a terrible book."

"I don't know . . . ," said Izzy, choking.

"It must be the worst book in the whole library."

Izzy sniffed.

"A dreadful book. Let me see the cover."

Izzy showed him.

"Ah. The internal combustion engine. A subject which has brought saints and mighty soldiers to their knees in despair."

Izzy smiled weakly.

"My name is Mr. Arrensen," said the man, extending his hand. "I'm the librarian."

Izzy took the long hand. It felt gray, and unexpectedly dry, like the skin of a snake. "I'm Izzy."

"Which is short for what?"

"For nothing. Just Izzy."

"Nonsense. Your name is Isaiah. I see in your response to the internal combustion engine that you have some foreknowledge of the Babylonian Exile. And you are right. The temple is going to be destroyed."

*　*　*

Izzy searched through the drawers in the wall until he found a map of the Annex, a small neighborhood close to the center of town. He found his house in this map. He pointed it out.

"Our house had been a duplex," he said. "Two houses, joined at a central wall. My parents bought one half, and then when they had paid off the mortgage they bought the other. An architect was hired to puncture the wall and make the house whole. He was an architect with ideas. Before commencing, he gathered the family together and read a quotation from Freud."

Here Izzy turned to the door, away from my desk, and began to recite the quotation from memory.

"In mental life nothing which has once been formed can perish. . . . Let us try to grasp what this assumption involves by taking an analogy from another field. We will choose as an example the history of the Eternal City."

He was turned away from me, so he could not see the color of my face.

"Let us . . . suppose that Rome is not a human habitation but a psychical entity . . . in which nothing that has once come into existence will have passed away and all the earlier phases of development continue to exist alongside the latest one. . . . In the place occupied by the Palazzo Caffarelli would once more stand—without the Palazzo having to be removed—the Temple of Jupiter Capitolinus."

The architect built for us a house with this fantastical notion in mind: he wanted to preserve every piece of

22

the house that had ever been, including those that he would have to destroy in the renovation, and those that had been destroyed long ago by the previous owners. He did research into the neighborhood, intending to resurrect all the buildings that had previously occupied the site of our house.

This house, he said, will be a place of memory. You will live in it while your family has a story to be remembered. Should you choose to forget that story, then the house will fall in upon itself, a victim of its own impossible foundations.

But, he said, there is something in the collapse of a house that drives this memory into the earth. When the house is gone, you will be able to read its story in the ruins.

While he spoke, the architect absentmindedly sketched a window on a torn piece of vellum, and in the corner of that window drew a small creature, chewing with noise and sharp teeth on a large dragonfly.

"Who are you?" asked Katie, surprised but unfrightened.

The creature said nothing, but chewed with relish, its eyes large and pale and blinking slowly.

"How did you get here?"

It was a long way from the windowsill to the ground below, but the creature looked as if it could climb. It had strong fingers, long and sharp; the middle finger was unusually long and skeletal, perhaps twice as long as the others. It pointed this finger at Katie, a casual gesture, and she felt the waters of spring dry in her throat and the trees moving in the window tighten into bones and crack. She tried to ask another question, but her throat had closed over in thirst. She coughed.

The twisted one spoke for her.

"Welcome," it said. "This is Katie's room. Anything born in the ravine is welcome here."

Something in Katie wanted to respond to this. "No," it wanted to say. "No!"

I became interested in predators. Predators and scavengers, but mostly predators. This is not so unusual in primary school; Mr. Arrensen had collected an entire shelf of animal books for precisely this reason. I was interested in a different kind of predator, however. There were only a few books devoted to birds, and none exclusively to birds of prey. I had become interested in raptors.

When Mr. Arrensen found me huddled over a plate in the Williams and Arlott *Field Guide to the Birds of East Africa,* he was disturbed.

" 'Secretary Bird, Vultures, and Lammergeyer.' Why that page in particular, Isaiah?"

I did not know, precisely. The secretary bird was interesting enough. It survived on a diet of poison: green and black mambas, spitting cobras, "noxious rodents." And vultures were vultures. But the lammergeyer. There was a bird. I had never heard of the lammergeyer. Even Aaron had never heard of the lammergeyer.

"Not gregarious," says the *Field Guide.* "Has the remarkable habit of dropping bones from a height to fracture them and eat the marrow.

"The most easily observed pair of lammergeyers in

Kenya are the pair which have made their home on the cliffs of Hell's Gate."

I talked about lammergeyers incessantly, for months. Finally I met somebody who had actually seen one. One of my father's friends was a land developer in Nairobi, and he had been told stories about the lammergeyer when he was a child. "The lammergeyer," he said, "will steal a baby from an unwatched cradle."

I could see the wings, pumping slowly but with great power to carry the burden into the equatorial sky, and the mother at her cradle, empty, and the moment of recognition.

It is always too late.

Sapphire would go out at least once yearly to become pregnant in the ravine. After some time she would deposit a brood of blind puppies in her basket on the basement floor. She would guard them ferociously. Sapphire, you see, had been raised in the shadow of the birds in the ravine. Nothing was going to carry one of her progeny away.

The basement was most readily accessible to Aaron, whose room lay at the top of the back stairs. As I have said, the architect did not simply cut holes in the wall when he rendered our duplex a single house. He built a city. Specifically, it was a twin city, a divided city, like walled Berlin or divided Jerusalem. The partition wall was punctured but left mostly intact. Winding corridors and crawl spaces were elaborated; rooms were made remote and inaccessible. Only the ground floor was public.

Aaron's room was the least accessible of all. The par-

25

ents lived on one side of the partition and the children on the other, but Aaron lived almost in another house. He had immediate access to the roof and the basement, but it was a long route to the kitchen.

Because of his location and allegiance to the dog, Aaron made it his business to keep an eye on the puppies. He would creep up and down the back stairs every few hours. From my room I could hear the stairs creak, and I knew that Aaron was in the basement at four in the morning.

If we did begin to disintegrate as a family, the problem may well have been architectural. Discipline, for instance, was always a problem with Aaron. He lived so far away that it was hard to know what he was up to, so my parents were forced to leave him be. Josh and I were also remote, though discipline only became an issue in my case somewhat late, and was never a problem with Josh. Nevertheless, we were far away.

The shape of the house conspired against us in other ways. My parents, for instance, lived in separate rooms, at either end of a tortuous corridor. My father was a light sleeper and had to be alone. I had no idea until much later that this was considered unusual in Toronto.

Izzy sighed. "I suppose I have to tell you something about my parents. I have to deal with them sooner or later, and with Sapphire in a basket on the basement floor nursing seven blind puppies, only one of which is blue, this is as good a time as any."

Which one of us was blue? That was the question, from the start, though we would not have put it that way.

Blue, moreover, would have to be the color of my mother, since it was her color that we wanted to be. On the surface, Josh was the blue one: my mother had fine red hair, and as I have said, this trait skipped both Aaron and me and surfaced in Joshua. The color that obsessed us, of course, without our knowing it, had nothing to do with what could be seen.

Aaron gave up earliest, I think. He chose at some point to be like my father, because my mother eluded him completely. I never gave up, properly, though I should probably have admitted defeat early on: Josh had inherited my mother's color; that should have been clear.

We were so distant from my parents that we could only study them as we might a difficult book or a distant climate. There was little conversation. Recently, when the news emerged in Vancouver that an entire community of children had kept the knowledge of a brutal murder from their parents for almost a year, I was not surprised. There is a white space, a linguistic rift between adults and children; that, at least, was the rule in my family.

Despite his distance, my father was transparent. He invariably knew precisely where he stood on any issue, and he did not have to spend much time figuring out his position. It had all been worked through and established by the time he left home at sixteen.

My mother stood even more resolutely, in the sense that she was implacable, but precisely where she stood was a cartographer's nightmare. My mother, you see, was unfathomable. She still is. She came from a long line of unfathomable people, and she retained this property without for a moment dispelling the illusion of a completely ordinary maternal existence.

My mother was Sarah Rachel Wolf by birth, but she married a Darlow, which erased a good part of her apparent ethnicity. In compensation, she insisted that the children be given good Old Testament names—mine was a compromise. She did not seem particularly religious, but what my mother seemed was generally irrelevant. What she in fact was, my father in particular so desperately wanted to know that he almost destroyed himself in the search.

Not that he made any great show of trying to find out. Though he spoke to her more than he spoke to us, it was rarely about anything important. But he would look at her once in a while with a look that wanted very much to be piercing. This was of course beyond him.

My father was caught up in the surface of things. The city of Toronto, which offers up its mystery only to the ungrateful and the dispossessed, can be very kind to those who do not ask questions. My father had made a point of forgetting, early, how to ask real questions. My father made no waves. He made buildings that changed the skyline so that the city would never look the same again on postcards. But he did not rock the boat.

This trained complacency left him unprepared for any proper attempt to understand my mother.

He was not very Jewish, either, by the time he had learned how to belong to the city. He had become reserved and polite, qualities that are considered typically Canadian by those who do not spend much time with Italians, Armenians, or Jews.

Izzy sank briefly into silence, strangely overcome. I could see that it was hard for him to discuss his family.

"Our concern, in this city of mediocrity—everyone's concern, though they don't know it any better than we do—is to find the story. To find the story and tell it, tell it well and remember it, so that we won't be forced to crawl back into the ravine. So that we won't be abandoned by our mother because we do not share her color. So that we won't be forced to search for our anonymous father, whose joy in our existence was limited wholly to our conception."

I understood this, perhaps better than Izzy could understand. What I knew of my own story was gone. It had been taken from me, some two years ago, by an event I could not remember. It was with great discomfort, then, that I listened to Izzy describe the first time he had an indication that Josh had found it, had tapped into it, was telling precisely this: the story I had lost.

My mother was oddly happy at dinner. She admired herself in the reflection of the microwave door, running her fingers through her hair; she smiled to herself as she went from the table to the stove and back again. We were having lamb, which was Joshua's favorite; he would drown the meat in mint sauce until it was almost candy. Josh too appeared oddly buoyant, even for a lamb dinner. Aaron was usually quiet at meals, as was my father.

"Path the lamb pleathe," Josh would pipe up every few minutes. And then: "Th'good."

Our table was a vast surface of walnut, pockmarked by accidents with forks and glasses. We generally had dinner off the good china, which was white with an elaborate metallic trim.

"Josh has news," my mother said, and we were all attentive.

"Th'nothing," Josh mumbled. "Path the lamb, pleathe."

"I spoke to his teacher this afternoon. She phoned."

Josh was in summer school; he had been ill off and on for a few months during the year and he was catching up. He was a good student, but he steadfastly refused to speak in class because of his lisp.

"Mrs. Marler said Josh got up in front of the whole class and told a story."

This was news. Josh blushed.

"He was a sensation. The kids clapped for ten minutes."

"Th'nothing . . ."

Aaron was excited. "What kind of story did you tell?"

"Jutht a thtory . . ."

"About what, jerk?"

"I made it up. Everybody wath thpothed to tell a thtory, and I wathn't going to do it, tho I didn't prepare anything, but then I did it anyway, tho I had to make it up."

"Sounds like it was pretty good," my father said.

"It wath okay."

Aaron was impressed. "And you got a standing ovation?"

Joshua rolled his eyes. "They didn't thtand."

None of us was unmoved by the significance of this small event: it marked a beginning in Joshua's life.

The creature disappeared as quickly as it had arrived, and the twisted one never spoke again, but Katie was changed. Though she remained in her mind invulnerable, she was never again entirely at ease. Whereas before she had been happy with what she had, now there was always the sense of something unfulfilled, something precarious, as if the boundaries to her world had become less stable. The ravine had been invited in.

Now, when she turned on the tap, there was sediment in the water: soil from the shadows outside her window. In the daylight, for the first time, she saw dark pinpricks circling in the sky far above. Who knew what they were, what they might prove to be, should they descend? They were not seagulls.

She began to bleed with the circling moon.

Sapphire would no longer let anyone near the blind puppies. Even Aaron had to check on them from a distance. She was reverting to her murderous state; she did not know or trust us.

Aaron was often late for meals now. He would sit in the basement, at some distance from the basket, and stare at the mewling family. He would forget where he was and lose track of the time. Sometimes he would even miss breakfast.

We had learned to start without him, though it always felt peculiar. Meals were the only time our family gathered; it was our gesture towards being one body.

Nevertheless, Aaron would do what he wished, and there was no taming him.

That was why we were not surprised to see his seat empty on that morning. My mother placed a bowl in front of his chair, in case he should arrive before breakfast was over, but nobody made an effort to call him.

Breakfast was mostly silent. We would each take a piece of the newspaper and make a show of reading, if only to hide the truth that we had nothing to say to each other. Nobody noticed Aaron, standing in the middle of the kitchen. He might have been standing there for a long time, before my mother looked up.

He looked at the same time dazed and angry, and he held a puppy in his hands like a votive offering.

"Aaron?" my mother inquired.

Joshua pushed aside his bowl and ran over to peer at the small dog curled up in Aaron's hands. Aaron did not look at him; he simply stood there.

Joshua turned with a hand over his mouth. "The puppy'th dead!"

The entire family was instantly on its feet and swarming about Aaron and the tiny corpse, neither of whom seemed to care, nor even to notice. It was the blue one.

I had never seen Aaron stricken before—perhaps none of us had—and it was a humbling sight. He allowed us to circle and make noises for a minute or so, and then he walked slowly out of the kitchen and up the stairs, still cradling the tiny creature as if it might wake. Nobody dared follow him.

As we quieted to a hush, an unmistakable noise welled up from the basement: Sapphire was crying.

Aaron did not go to school that day. Nor did he leave his room. Nor did he relinquish the corpse.

Katie began to notice the details of her room for the first time. She saw that the snake carved into the frame of her mirror was the same snake that curled around the legs of her bed. She saw that the furniture, which she had always thought was a stained mahogany veneer, was in truth solid ebony. She realized this when she tried to move the bed; it was so heavy that it cut into the floor.

Katie began to think about her grandmother, whom she had never met. Her grandmother had married at fifteen. She had moved with her new husband to the land he had inherited: a tea plantation in East Africa. Katie imagined what it must have been like to leave the English countryside for that tangled world.

This mysterious furniture had been carved for her grandmother's bedroom in Africa. She had died before Katie was born, and her daughter—Katie's mother— had paid a huge sum to have the furniture shipped to Canada.

Katie's mother had never been able to sleep in the bed; the dreams were overwhelming.

Katie had the same dreams, but she did not mind them. She dreamed of black hands rubbing oil into the legs of the chairs, and curling them like baobabs. She dreamed of an empty cradle, and of a bird carrying her up and beyond the confines of the Rift Valley, so that she could stare into the red landscape.

The curtains were also from the plantation. They were

twisted by hand out of some diaphanous material into a pattern of flowers and vines. Katie stared into them for the first time, and began to understand how foreign these flowers were: nothing like them would ever grow in her garden.

Her family, which she had always taken for granted, now seemed old and mysterious. She spent hours in front of the mirror, trying to divine her ancestors. Her eyes were pale and myopic, an equatorial color that she had from the sky of her grandmother. The whole family was blond, but Katie's hair also curled about her in a way that was unfamiliar. She held the long hair in front of her hands and thought: Where does this come from, this part of me that is dead?

I too would study the line of Katie's hair and wonder: Who drew this, and why does it draw me so?

It was difficult to know what Aaron was up to. My parents were torn. Should they insist that he bury the dog for reasons of decency and hygiene, or should they respect the privacy of his grief? Nobody had ever seen Aaron in this state, and it was unsettling. They could not decide between them what to do, so they waited.

It was a week later, when Aaron emerged from the coma, that we understood what had happened.

Joshua was the first to hear the story from Aaron's mouth. In his peculiar lisping manner, he related the tale to us, and what we derived from the difficult monologue was this.

Aaron had scaled the roof with an iron rod and a spool of wire under his arm—Aaron always seemed to have supplies of wire, steel, concrete, and pulleys. He climbed the television aerial, which was as tall again as the house itself, and fixed the rod to the top of the central mast. Around the base of the rod he wound a strip of wire, so that the copper formed a conductive path with the iron, then he trailed the wire down the aerial, across the roof, down the side of the house, and into his bathroom window. Aaron had his own bathroom beneath the eaves; it was even more isolated than his room.

The puppy, which had not even had the opportunity to open its eyes, lay curled in the sink. Aaron stripped the other end of the wire and wound it gently around the puppy's neck. Then he locked the door and sat on the edge of the tub, waiting for the storm.

The clouds had been gathering for three days. They drifted in from all directions, dark clouds, pieces of black; they came together until they were one cloud that obliterated the sky. A gray-yellow heaviness filled the air. The light was morbid, and everyone found that his bones ached. Aaron waited.

When the last cloud fell into place, Sapphire began to pull herself slowly up the stairs. She had holed up in the basement for days, crying, but now she sensed that the hour of reckoning was near. The blue puppy had been healthy when she went to sleep; when she awoke it was dead. Even in her wolf's mind she could sense the truth: she had smothered it, herself, while dreaming. Aaron waited.

Renegade clouds were rolling across the sky now, great electrical clouds, men-o'-war, trailing invisible tentacles of charged and dangerous air. Sapphire began to claw at the bathroom door, howling, but Aaron would not let her in. "Hang on, wolfling," he said cheerfully, "I'm going to bring your baby back to life." And he waited.

At last a long tentacle brushed against the iron rod. The metal ignited and melted and fused with the wire, which carried the charge across the roof and down the eaves and through the window and into the veins of the dead one, just as Sapphire clawed right through the door and howled to the sink and caught fire as the blast split the porcelain and melted the plumbing and sent Aaron sprawling charred and unconscious into the hard bathtub.

My parents were justifiably upset.

Aaron would heal without scars, but the puppies were now orphans and had to be fed with dropper bottles full of warm milk.

Aaron, however, was curiously unrepentant, and many months later we found out why. We were in a secret place—one of the few times Aaron ever allowed me the privilege of occupying one of these—and he had Josh and me sit very quietly as he told us what had happened. "It moved," he said. "Right when the lightning hit I swear the puppy came alive and looked at me." He paused and his eyes lit up. "It can be done."

Mr. Arrensen's lessons have come back to haunt me, now that it is too late. I have not seen him in many years. I wonder what he would think of me now. The last time I saw him, he did not think much of me, and I have changed even more since. He was very wise, but I doubt even he could imagine a human being could change so greatly. I understand now a part of what he was saying about Aaron: about arrogance, and excess, and the crime of the usurper.

I have taken to walking distances at night. Particularly after it has rained, I find the sidewalk calming. Headlights come up ahead of me and sparkle off the wetness of the road, and when the car passes, it is like the passing of a ghost.

I could dearly use a wise friend now.

It was years before the second visitor came. Katie had changed. She had become wild and joyous, and though she was considered peculiar, most girls wanted to be her friend. Most boys wanted something else from her, but she laughed at them, because they were young and clumsy and incapable of love.

Though she never had to be alone, she spent long stretches by herself, locked in her room. Since that night many years before, the twisted one had never said a word, and had gradually become less important in her life. It was now sitting in the closet, unhappily, in the company of those other dolls. The creature with the skeletal finger had disappeared into the ravine, and she had never seen it again.

The sediment in the water supply was now a constant problem, however. Her father could not understand it. The water was pumped into the ravine from a reservoir; nobody else who tapped into this reservoir had soil in their water.

The night the second visitor arrived, the pipes had seized up. Katie tried to brush her teeth, but nothing would come out of the tap except dust and webs and a small insect husk, curled and dried.

There were unfamiliar calls in the night air. Not seagulls, but something else. She curled up at the head of her bed, awake with expectation.

Katie looked down at her hands, examining a thumbnail. It had begun to grow crookedly. When she looked up again, he was there. He stood in her open window, which had been empty the moment before.

Izzy examined his own nails, which were long and discolored. There was now a pile of documents on the desk, relating to his story. We had mapped the narrative as he stumbled along, erratically; it helped. The story at the beginning was held together mostly by places; it took a long time before I could link the events. And even then, location was everything.

I was going to be late for my wedding. The phone began to ring, but I ignored it. At last I disconnected the cord from the wall.

Before you judge me too harshly, I should say something about the woman I was supposed to marry. I do not love her. We both understand that I owe her a great deal, but I have never professed to love her.

It is difficult to explain precisely what I owe to this woman. When she met me, two years ago, nobody else would have me. I would like to think that she remained open to me out of a certain generosity of spirit. This is what I have told myself, many times, in an effort to justify my impending marriage. It is, however, a lie.

She took me, when nobody else would have me, because she felt that in doing so she could own me completely.

She is not attractive, my fiancée, nor does she love me, but she knows that I owe her my life and will therefore be loyal. This puts me in a different category from most men. Most men, it seems, leave her.

They leave her when they discover the depth of her acquisitive spirit, how she wants to own everything as completely as a thing can be owned. I found myself appalled, as well, the first time I saw her stare at me with that smug look, the same look that I have seen her father evince in shopping malls.

Josh was staying out very late, and my parents were trying to assess whether this was a good thing. Not that they discussed it; they simply made efforts towards addressing the question, and depending upon the degree to which these efforts failed, they established an opinion. As far as I could tell, my mother was unperturbed by Josh's behavior; she seemed to have a sense that it was all right, whatever he was doing. My father, I think, took the generic stance that midnight was too late for a ten-year-old to be arriving home. I was twelve, which was different: twelve-year-olds could do what they wanted. And Aaron was a renegade, so the question did not properly apply to him. But Josh was still innocent and, we all assumed, relatively helpless.

I was interested in finding out what Josh was up to. He seemed to have a major project of his own, which did not include Aaron, and this was new. Aaron would sometimes inquire casually about Josh's disappearances, but Josh was not telling anybody.

I now understand the multiplication of secrets to be my mother's influence upon the family. It is as if we began as an organic whole, with intimate access to each other, and slowly the secrets grew like aisles and walls until we were each so different from the others that we would soon have to shout to make ourselves heard. It was my mother who did it.

My father, as I have said, was a straightforward man. He had a beard, which was admired by the community, and he made buildings, which was a proper way to spend time. He was known as a "developer," and this had a solid, modern ring to it. I did not know much about what he did back then. It was never discussed, but it allowed us to live in comfort, so I was content.

When I think back, I realize that we must have had considerably more money than my father ever spent. I never had the perception that we were rich, but we must have been: developers in Toronto have traditionally done very well. Nothing in Toronto is thought worthy of preservation, and growth is almost a religion. The aldermen, almost uniformly soft in taste and scruples, will do anything to increase the size of a building. I am told this has something to do with a corresponding increase in the size of campaign contributions; my father was always donating money to worthwhile political causes.

Because of his position in the community, my father could afford to be a public man. He enjoyed his reputation as an accessible if stern community leader, and would often appear as a figurehead at important events. When I was young, my mother would invariably go with him, and we children were often invited to these ceremonies as well. As time progressed, and it became apparent that I was drifting and that Josh would not stop lisping, we ceased to be invited. My mother too accompanied my father less and less, and I have my theories about this.

Mother did not enhance my father's appearance as a paragon of openness and civic loyalty. Her motivation was hidden, and quiet, and this made her suspect in the world of appearances. Certainly nobody was in a position to say anything scandalous about my mother or her family; the problem was that nobody was in a position to say anything whatsoever about them, and that made people nervous.

I am also convinced, although I could not back this up with much, that we all went our separate ways in search of a common goal: the unraveling of the maternal secret. Certainly we each sought the clue to a separate mystery, and this attraction to the dark and hidden must have come from somewhere.

My grandfather on my mother's side was a quiet man. He lived across the city to the east in a large apartment, and he would have us over to dinner once a month. His wife had died in childbirth, and he had been alone since my mother got married, but he did not appear lonely.

When we arrived for dinner, he would greet each of us with a tiny smile and lead us into the living room. Aaron was always ill at ease in Abba's apartment; everything was old and smelled of a distant continent, a continent of dust and carpets, red glass and memories, and it left him feeling alien. I was fascinated, however, by the walls covered in books whose titles I could not begin to read.

Of all of us, Josh had the best relationship with the old man. Neither spoke much, and neither felt any pressure to speak; they were reasonably content simply to be around each other.

Abba would cook chicken, with unfamiliar spices and cranberry sauce. At home we associated cranberry sauce with turkey, but then what did we know? He always laid out his best silver, and I seem to remember that the silverware had a story behind it—a story none of us had been told. My father would spend most of the evening trying to strike up serious conversations with either my grandfather or my mother, but Abba would only utter kind platitudes at the table, and my mother became silent and happy in his presence.

"So Dad," my father would say, "I understand real estate's booming in Scarborough. This property's going to become quite attractive."

"Yes, it's a nice apartment. I'm happy here. Would you like some more chicken?"

Katie, who had never known reason to fear anyone, lifted her head and smiled openly. He had walked straight through the open window, as if it were a door.

"Hello," she whispered.

He bowed his head graciously. Even as she told me the story, Katie could not recall how he was dressed. Or what he looked like, precisely: "He was like a beau-

tiful cat. Or a lion. But human. Or perhaps a wolf . . .
I'm not sure."

They spoke for hours, about what her life was like.
She had never thought about her life before, and this
added an element of reflection to her bright existence.
As they talked, she realized that she did not care about
herself at all. She cared about him. But he would not
say anything of himself, and he departed in the early
morning before the sun.

Katie lay still for a long time. She could not sleep,
although she was very tired, so at last she stood and
approached the mirror to comb her hair. And there on
the dresser was a tangle of roots, torn from some plant,
wet with the invisible water from the air.

She kept the roots in a bowl of water by the side of
her bed, and they neither grew nor died, but the room
was changed by them as if they had some wild potency,
so that even her waking hours rolled aimlessly like a
drunken sleep. Nor did the young man reappear that
night, nor the next, nor the next.

She refused to go downstairs. When her mother
questioned her, Katie murmured something about "loyalty."

Josh seemed unusually content with life during the days,
and in the evenings he would disappear. Once Father
caught him putting a tie on before he left.

"What's the tie for?"

"Jutht felt like wearing one."

Nobody ever expects his younger brother to become
an independent human being. It is not one of those

scheduled events. I found it exciting, not the least because it freed me from the tyranny of majority rule: Aaron and Josh still spent time together, but relations were strained. It seemed even Aaron was excluded from the secret.

I was surprised Aaron never thought to follow Josh some evening: I certainly felt no qualms about spying.

For a month Katie remained in her room and saw her psyche flower with the influence of the torn root. In her mind she completed the plant in a thousand ways, growing stems and branches and leaves, but never free of the phantom pain, the fact of severance. And then, one month to the night of his first visit, the visitor returned.

Again, he stepped through the window as Katie lay upon the bed, her eyes closed and her whole being concentrated on her loneliness. This time he placed a hand upon her head, and she opened her eyes at his touch.

He sat on the edge of the bed and spoke to her without saying anything, and she answered saying even less.

She felt foolish, dressed as she was in her thick dressing gown, so she removed it as they spoke, and lay naked on the surface of her giant bed. He did not touch her, nor did he even look at her lovely pale limbs, which no man had ever seen; he merely stared into her eyes and spoke.

Katie felt the feet of the bed tremble; the frame of the mirror was hissing like a black mamba, and the curtains moved in the wind like a garden full of alien flowers.

She put a hand to her breast to measure her heart, which she felt was on the verge of either singing or stopping, and another hand between her thighs because she was empty like a well. But her eyes remained alive and her voice was sweet and strong. Only when he left did she fall back upon the bed in a fever, burning where his hand had touched her forehead.

Katie's mother found her the next morning in this position, naked and trembling. She pulled a blanket over her daughter, phoned for a doctor, and tipped a long green stem into the bowl with the roots.

A crisis was brewing at home. Aaron was building dangerous machines in his room, with stolen materials, and my parents were turning a blind eye. They no longer seemed capable of orchestrating the necessary confrontation: my father would try to arrange a meeting, and just as Aaron entered the room my mother would rise and glide out the door. This left my father with little stomach for the disciplinary hearing; he would mumble something banal and leave. Aaron would often stay in the room, smiling, as if to say: Where's my comeuppance? You owe me.

We were tragedians in flapping rubber shoes.

What had happened? Perhaps in time the true severity of the incident with the wolf cub had become fully apparent to all, as had the embarrassing inability of my parents to come together in punishment. Aaron felt unlike a child, and subject to no one; my parents felt unlike parents. And I began to realize that were I to go astray, there would be no one to correct me. It was a breathless recognition: the vertigo of absolute freedom. It did me no good whatsoever.

Often the lights in the house would fail all at once, and in the hushed darkness we could hear an electrical hum in Aaron's room: something mechanical was striving for life.

Josh alone was permitted to visit the place. He would make cryptic, lisping pronouncements, which made us wonder all the more what was happening in the furthest corner of the house.

"He'th making thingth," Josh would say. "They're gedding bigger."

For a week Katie lay in a delirium, but she did not seem to suffer physically: she neither lost weight nor grew pale. She simply dreamed feverish dreams, preferring to remain unconscious in the absence of her visitor. In one particularly vivid dream a stooped man in a black hood led a procession down the center of a city street. The cars to either side were stopped in their tracks, and their occupants were draped out of the windows with their eyes closed, as if the plague had swept suddenly through rush-hour traffic. The procession was murky and difficult to discern, a cloud of poisonous smoke, but the tall hunched leader was sharp and black like a piece of cut obsidian. Katie stood on her doorstep and waited until the procession turned the corner and began to wend its doleful way up her street. She was naked, and blushing. When the procession was about to pass her house, the leader held up his hand, and the shadowy line froze. He stepped clear of them and approached the doorstep, where he knelt with his head so close that Katie could feel his breath. Without showing his face, he put a white hand inside his cloak and drew out a single white rose. Blushing even more deeply, Katie took the stem between two fingers and touched the flower with her other hand. Her breath disappeared in pain. The petals were so cold that they burned her fingertips, and as she held the flower to her nose, an arctic storm boiled through the street and drowned the dream in quiet white.

The doctor told Katie's mother that he could do nothing for her; he insisted the spell was psychological, and that she might perhaps like to see a therapist when she emerged from the fever. Katie's mother spent hours at the foot of her daughter's bed, trying to pierce her dreams.

But Katie remained in her cocoon until a month had passed. She woke from her fever just in time to see the visitor step from the air to her windowsill.

This time they did not speak, but Katie allowed the man to open her robe and touch her; wherever his fingertips met her skin a blood-red mark would appear for a moment and then fade. He touched her neck and shoulders, and then her stomach. When at last he touched her breasts, she felt sick with longing, but he closed her robe, pressed his fingers to her lips, and departed.

Katie turned over and held her pillow to her face and wept.

When she finally arose from her bed, she noticed a curled leaf on the night table. The leaf had red veins, and its form was oddly human and disturbing. It seemed to match some image from her dreams, but it had no scent. After floating the leaf on the bowl that contained the roots and the stem, she went to the window to stare at the sky. Briefly, she considered stepping out after him, and she put her fingers to her lips where he had touched her.

In the morning she discovered that she could not speak.

Josh was strangely silent at dinner. He ate his food quickly and then stared with intensity at the empty plate. It was as if he were trying to work something out in his head, or were running over something he had memorized. When my father spoke to him, he did not notice, and when my father spoke again, more insistently, Josh looked up from his plate with an expression of annoyance: Why are you interrupting me?

I sensed it might be an appropriate night to follow my little brother on his evening travels.

After dinner, he excused himself quickly and went to his room. I waited in the living room, with a view of the front door, and pretended to read a book.

In an hour, Josh came quietly downstairs, wearing a tie. He looked at me to ascertain that I was deeply engrossed in my book, then let himself carefully out the front door.

I waited a minute. Then I slipped out the door and scanned the street. Josh was walking quickly down the sidewalk, apparently deep in thought, because he never took his eyes from the pavement in front of him. I felt secure moving quietly behind him.

We were walking mostly to the south. On our streets the houses were large, and the trees were still thick before the onslaught of Dutch elm disease. We walked into an area almost barren of trees, where the houses were tall and thin and joined in twos. They had been painted garish colors by the Chinese and the Portuguese. We passed a tiny synagogue, smaller than a house, from the days when this had been a Jewish neighborhood. Josh never hesitated. He led me through a bewildering tangle of narrow roads and tiny parks until we were in a new residential district, where the thin houses had been renovated into bright, childlike homes trimmed in pine and wrought iron. We crossed every significant neighborhood in the area.

Josh spoke constantly as he walked, as if he were rehearsing a story, or a speech. Sometimes he would stop speaking and stare about him to get his bearings; the shape of the city seemed to remind him of what he was to say next. Then he would start to speak again, and I would shadow him, quietly, as we made our way.

I could never hear properly what he was saying. The few words I could catch, though, left me with the uneasy feeling that Josh was telling a story, and that the story was not his own. He stopped in the middle of the road, for instance, and stood on a manhole cover: here he recited some words that sounded perhaps like Shakespeare. Later, he stood in front of one of the hospitals on University Avenue and as he stared up at a lit window, he said something mournful. Again, I could not hear him properly, but I caught the name "Katie," spoken with remorse.

We walked for hours.

It was only when we were within a few blocks of our house that I understood the nature of our path: Josh had led me in a circle.

He disappeared into the house and repaired immediately to his room. When I innocently knocked on his door some minutes later to see what he was doing, he had no time for me: he was busy writing copious notes on foolscap sheets.

Aaron was growing at a fierce rate. He was already a head taller than me, and he seemed bent upon widening the gap. Also, though I was still desperately thin (the general condition of our birth), Aaron was developing the chest of a leopard and prominent veins on his arms.

My father was a strong man as well; he had been a wrestler of some skill at university, and I believe he had given up all hope of having children who were anything more than matchsticks. In fact, it was Aaron's new physique that began to effect a reconciliation between the two.

Neither spoke to the other any more than before, but there was a benevolent look in Father's eyes whenever Aaron arrived downstairs for breakfast. Father would occasionally make suggestions regarding Aaron's diet, and Aaron would nod his head, as if he thought whatever was said was a good idea. Since he had failed to deal properly with his son as a child, Father now had hopes that he might have a premature adult with whom he could establish things anew.

As for me, I hardly felt this large creature was my brother. I did not know Aaron at all; we had never really spoken, and now his physical presence was so new that he might well have been a visitor. Overwhelmingly, however, I was beginning to realize that the visitor to the family was not Aaron, nor Josh. It was me.

I watched them all as if they were pictures behind glass. And it is true that sometimes as I stared at my family over dinner they would lose their solidity, and the color would drain from them until they were flat against the wall of my vision like a sepia print.

I occupied a different realm.

Katie's mother was bending beneath the weight of her daughter's transformation. To have Katie awake, but no more communicative than when she had been feverish, was an impossible irony, and Katie's mother had no idea whom to consult. Psychotherapy seemed out of the question: not only could Katie not speak but she could not write or do anything to indicate her thoughts, and psychotherapists are not fond of doing any, never mind all, of the talking.

Long days were spent with Katie and her mother sitting on the bed and staring at each other, Katie mute and her mother mutely weeping.

And the three torn gifts, which now approached something complete but broken, continued to assert their presence in the room, each coloring another dimension of Katie's thoughts. The roots grew outward, winding their way about the room like the path through a complex garden, an asymmetrical garden in which the hand of the gardener is apparent only to the most subtle theologian. The pale stem grew upward, doomed and frail; it put the dread of winter into the air, so that the season was shown to be ephemeral and thus more desperately beautiful. And the curled leaf peopled the psyche with writhing shapes: bodies turned away and twisting in chains, pollinating lovers trying to breathe in every piece of the garden's influence.

How many more gifts will I receive? And will they somehow be made whole? These were Katie's most urgent thoughts.

Nor was her mother unaware of the influence: entering Katie's room was like entering a greenhouse without glass, a cube of denser atmosphere floating inside the common air of the surrounding house.

Josh began to sing. It was a shock to the family, a tremor through the structure of the house; nobody had ever sung there before. My mother would occasionally hum some remote melody but she would start well into it and finish midway through a phrase, so it was never properly music except insofar as it was completed inside her head. Josh, however, was singing whole songs. From beginning to end.

He did not seem to care who listened; he simply liked to fill the air with his voice. We were so amazed that none of us noticed for the longest time that something even more remarkable was occurring: when Josh sang, his lisp disappeared. He could sing an entire lyric and articulate every syllable without once transmuting a consonant into that thick-tongued beast that would sit on his lip and fall wounded to the floor.

Josh now disappeared nightly. I no longer had the nerve to follow. He seemed to be dancing towards the light, while I circled earthward. If anything, I felt I had more and more in common with Aaron, and the sounds that leaked through the walls of his room spoke more to me than Josh's singing.

Nevertheless, I longed to know what Josh was about. What kind of story was he telling as he circled? Why did he clip on a tie, as if it were a formal occasion? Was he always alone? The name Katie had lodged in my memory, and I could not call it to mind without thinking about the ravine, about predators and prey.

I began to understand that there were circles in the sky, and circles down below. The moon circled obliviously. The birds in the ravine would fly to the outer reaches of sight and then circle the city. Josh walked in circles, singing. The moon was held in its circle by gravity, the birds by hunger, and Josh by something else.

One night, when Josh clipped his tie onto his clean shirt, I resolved to follow him again.

We took precisely the same route as before. He spoke, this time much more clearly, and sang in his perfect soprano voice, which had the timbre of a sine wave in a belfry. The wind was so high that I did not hear the precise words; yet something was happening to the city around us as we walked.

The pillars holding up porches in front of houses would take on female form, and the roof above them would be too heavy for their now human arms. I never had the strength to watch as one of these porches collapsed, crushing its female support, but I heard the cries. We left a trail of ruins behind us.

The seagulls swarmed in the sky above. When I was very young, the seagulls in Toronto remained at the waterfront. Every year they began to usurp more and more of the city, until they had become a nuisance as far away as the airport; they would be caught in the engines of jets on the runway, miles from Lake Ontario.

The gulls were now a familiar sight inland, but I had never seen this many at night.

The next morning I walked past some of the houses whose porches had fallen the night before and was amazed to find them whole, the pillars no longer women but mute columns, topped with concrete capitals, spilling over with acanthus leaves.

There was an entire section of the library that I had avoided until now. Mr. Arrensen had never precisely guided me in my reading, although he had reacted to certain tendencies with dismay or with quiet approval. We had never discussed this one section. I had never shown interest in these books, and he had never suggested that I might. My home, however, was splitting in two, moving in two separate directions, and I wanted for the first time to understand what was happening.

Aaron was building a machine. He spent long afternoons in the ravine where he had found Sapphire. He

54

was studying the environment. He was trying to determine the conditions under which an animal might be brought to life. Aaron used this research in the construction of his project, though I had only the vaguest sense of what that project signified.

Josh was moving in the opposite direction. He was singing peculiar songs, which we could not understand, but I had followed him in his travels, and I had seen what happened to the buildings around him as he sang.

Where Aaron was building, Josh was singing the story of ruins. Aaron was dreaming of a new empire, the birth of a new regime, and Josh was already telling the story of its demise. Aaron was trying to forget what had come before; he was trying to begin with a tabula rasa; he was making something new. Josh was forcing him to remember.

Izzy was unhappy now, telling the story of how his family began to divide from itself. "The cracks began to appear. Everything threatened to split in two: the house, my parents, my brothers . . . myself."

He looked at me, and I felt vaguely nauseated, conspiratorial, as if I had participated in this schism in some horrible but integral way.

"I told Mr. Arrensen that my brother was spending days in the ravine, trying to discover the seeds of creation. I explained that he had never forgotten his experiment with the blue puppy, that he was building a machine in his room, that I did not know much about it, except that it seemed to be a much more sophisticated version of his attempt with the aerial and the lightning rod."

Mr. Arrensen gave me a book to read, about a man who attempted to create life in the laboratory. "This is a book about the modern project," he said. "Almost everything that we do, in this century, is at base a variant of this project: the attempt to reduce the mystery of nature to a process that can be understood, and repeated, and tamed."

I told him about Josh, and the circling story, and the buildings that had become human and then collapsed.

"That," he said, "is the same story."

I did not understand.

"We build," he said. "We build, and we are successful, and then we forget in our arrogance that what we have built is merely our own: it rests on a structure of human frailty; it is already on the path towards its own ruin.

"Your brother Josh is simply singing the complete circle, from arrogance, to transgression, to destruction.

"The first bitter story ever told was precisely this one; the crime of the usurper. We pretend to knowledge that is not rightfully ours. We make something, believing that we have mastered what we have merely stolen. Finally, what we make takes vengeance upon us, and we are forced to confront the truth, which is in fact no different from the original mystery: that we know very little."

I read the story about the man who tried to create human life and produced instead a monster. But I did not stop there.

"If Mr. Arrensen were right," said Izzy, "then this story had found its way into the fabric of the century.

The arrogance, the transgression, and the vengeance. I wanted to know about this, because I felt that this same drama was being played out, on a smaller scale, in my own family. I turned for the first time to the place in the library where this story was told."

I was twelve years old. The story I read is not one that can be assimilated at any age. At twelve, however, there is no hope.

They were books of history. Simple history. The telling of a human story, the gathering of honest perspectives, the attempt to say what happened, and perhaps why. That was all I was reading.

Written history ought to be relatively innocuous. Fiction is unbounded. The infinite potency of the human mind to create horror on a blank page would result, you would think, in the more palpable terror. History suffers from constraints. It must have been real. It must have been capable of happening.

I began to understand, however, that history has authors. That creative men with the imaginative powers of Artaud and Bataille do not always confine themselves to fiction; that they can, if they are very gifted, write their script in flowing agony across the flesh of nations. And the horror that has happened is always, always more appalling than the horror that has not, simply by virtue of having happened.

It is not such a peculiar thing to read these books at the age of twelve. Any moderately precocious child can take these books off the shelf; they are there to be read. Some of them are in very simple language. The mere sequence of events is quite simple to grasp. The significance, of course, can never be grasped. We will die and never know what these simple events mean; but the events themselves are all too ordinary.

I read a story about a man with a wonderful voice.

There was a man with a wonderful voice. When he spoke, people listened, and what he had to say touched them to the core. "We can overcome what we are," he said. "We can remake ourselves in our own image. We can take our destiny into our hands, and shape its course."

There was, at the same time, a group of people with an ancient book. They lived in the same land as the man with the wonderful voice. The ancient book, however, which was a book of memory, said precisely the opposite thing from the man with the wonderful voice.

"Man was not made to overcome what he is," said the book.

The book told a circular story. A story that repeated itself, over and over, so that every part of the book contained within itself the entire book. The story was this.

A group of men become arrogant. Why should we not build a tower to the heavens, they ask. If we build a tower to the heavens, then we will become like gods. This is the beginning of the story.

The foundations are laid. Men—slaves—die in the laying of the foundations, and are buried in hollow stones in the wall of the tower. The dead men hold the tower up, and it begins to grow. This is the middle of the story.

One day, when the tower is on the verge of completion, when it is so tall that the men on the ramparts can almost reach out and touch the fringe of heaven, the sky becomes black and fills with terrible light. There is the sound of bones cracking.

Those at the base of the tower see this: for the moment, the great stones in the foundation disappear. In their place, briefly resurrected, are the slaves. They now hold the tower up, in place of the stones.

The slaves have become human pillars. The entire tower rests briefly upon the hands of these slaves.

There is the sound of bones cracking.

The muscles strain and give out. The spines snap. The slaves are crushed and again entombed in the foundations of the tower, which is now a ruin. The men who built the tower are divided from each other and scattered across the face of the earth, but in the destruction of the tower is engendered the beginning of a story. The tale is remembered, and written, and told. This is the beginning and the end of the story.

The man with the wonderful voice was aware of this story. He was aware that this story was written in the book, and he knew that he could not allow such a story to be remembered and told. He understood that the story was disheartening, that it cast aspersions upon his own eloquent project. He began therefore to engineer the great forgetting.

To forget is hard work. He knew this. But to forget is to be free.

This is what he did, to implement the great forgetting.

The members of the group who owned and read the book were placed in cattle cars and taken to another place. Here mothers were separated from their children, because as everybody knows children cannot work, and mothers still have work left in them. Fathers, too, were put to work, but since they could work even better they were put somewhere else again.

The sick, who are like children and cannot work, were naturally separated off as well. One man did the separating, because it is an easy thing to do. He simply pointed: you go that way, and work; you go that way, and do not.

Those who did not work suffered less. Work, it was said, made men free, and it is true that some of these who worked were at last set free.

Of the ones who did not work, some went without pain. They were told that they were going to be washed, which was a good thing, because in the ride they had become filthy. The pipes, however, did not have water in them, and the showerheads did not spray water.

Some were permitted to live. They did service to science—to the field of medicine, in particular—so that others could benefit from their suffering.

In this way, the man with the wonderful voice ensured that the book was almost forgotten, and the world slowly changed.

It changed for the group who had owned the book. On the day that freedom was granted, the group was examined, and found to be much smaller than it had been before.

It changed for other people as well. Many of these,

before the eloquent man began to speak so well, had a good idea why they were doing what they did, and many of them had a healthy regard for mankind. On the day that freedom was granted, and the group was revealed in its altered condition, many people felt the change. It was no longer simply a matter of carrying on. You could not simply go home. Home did not seem to exist. Or if it did, it hardly mattered.

Nothing, in fact, made much sense in the light of this new day. "We have done something," the people said, "and it cannot be undone." Even those who had done nothing could not separate themselves entirely from those who had done something, because, as the saying goes, "We are all human." Something had been allowed to occur that was different, and in light of this everything had changed.

Everybody wanted proof. They wanted some proof that would convince them that they were somehow different in kind from the young man with the splendid voice. It did not suffice that they were different in some important way; they had to be different in kind. "If he was human," many said, "then I do not want to be human too."

But, as the saying goes, "We are all human."

For many people, because of the great effort to forget that one book, no books ever made sense again.

Izzy looked into my eyes, pleading.

"Do you understand?" he said. "I was twelve years old. Certainly what I suffered, simply reading about this, was nothing. This was part of the suffering: the recognition that I had no right to suffer, because I was simply reading about this. It had not happened to me.

"Do you understand?"

I looked away.

"What was I supposed to do?" he said. "My first thought was to forget, to put it out of my mind—'May his name and memory be erased'—but part of me rejected this as obscene. What right do I have to forget the suffering of others?"

I did not know. But as I have said, I have had my problems with memory, and I began to feel sick.

"But then, I was twelve years old. And to remember this, from the age of twelve onwards—to carry the knowledge of this in my mind for the rest of my life, seemed unbearable. What was I supposed to do?

"I make this sound very rational. I was, of course, much less rational at the time. My mind was moving in all sorts of perverse ways, desperate ways. I was twelve years old.

"The most urgent need, at that time, was to divorce myself from the man with the wonderful voice. If there was anything like him in me—any part of me that was in any way like that man—I wanted it gone. I wanted to cut it from myself and throw it away.

"I remember this, distinctly. My wish to cut myself away from myself. I think it had something to do with what happened that evening."

Upon returning home, my immediate thought was that Aaron's machine had to be stopped. I now saw it for what it was: an attempt to tame the mysteries of the ravine.

Aaron was trying to build a tower to heaven, so that he could steal the source of life and bring it back down to earth. This was what Mr. Arrensen meant by the arrogance of the usurper. I was determined to stop him.

When I entered his room he was not there. I looked about me; I had not been inside this room since he began work on the machine.

It was dark. Aaron had covered the windows, but I could hear the sound of a great wheel turning, and soon I began to make out shapes.

There were open boxes of soil that he had carried back from the ravine. On each of these lay a dead animal, curled up. They were mournful and silent, each lying on its own bed of soil. These too he must have found in the ravine, but I had never seen him bring one home. In the far wall of the room was the project itself.

It was built right into the wall. The great wheel turned, and as it turned it made an unearthly noise. The room felt as if it were an organic whole, connected in some vital way to the turning of that wheel. The wheel was the heart of the room.

I could not understand the machine. It was far too complex. Nevertheless, as I stared at it I could make out certain features. I knew the wheel must be the heart. And I knew that the two poles standing in front of the wheel must be the termini.

It was built in such a way that this was obvious: the entire room full of machinery was oriented towards those two poles. They were the object of all this complexity. They were the goal.

The poles were not impressive. They stood about three feet apart, fixed into the floor. Wires ran from the base of each into the machine built into the wall. Each was capped with a small shining sphere of metal.

Between these spheres, on a wooden platform, was a box of soil. There was no animal on this box.

The poles were thin. I could not tell what they were made of, but I thought to myself: quite possibly I could bend these out of shape, maybe even twist them together; this might damage the machine in some irreparable way. I was determined to try.

From behind me, a dog began to bark. I looked back and could see a cage in the corner of the room. A small dog was straining at the bars. Its eyes were white and clouded, as if in death.

I stepped carefully up to the poles and stood in front of them. I could tell, somehow, that the air between them was not like the air in the rest of the room. There was nothing visible, but I could sense it: the air between those shining termini was different.

I kicked the wooden platform out of the way. The box fell, the soil scattered in an arc across the floor. I stepped between the poles and grabbed a sphere with either hand. As I felt the shine of the metal, I heard Aaron's voice from the door: "Izzy! Don't touch that!"

But it was too late. I had become a circuit.

Izzy stood up. He paced about my office, full of strange energy. I stared at my watch; my wedding was to start in ten minutes. He continued his story.

"I knew something was different, from that moment

on. Aaron pulled me away from the machine; he was angry, and nervous, but he insisted that I had not been harmed in any way. I knew, though, that something was different.

"At dinner that night I had such a horrible pain in my stomach that I could not eat. My mother repeatedly asked Aaron what his machine was for, and what had happened to me, but he would not say.

" 'Don't worry,' said Aaron, 'he'll be fine.'

"Josh was silent throughout dinner, but at the very end he answered my mother's question, in a small voice filled with awe. He told her what Aaron's machine was designed to do. I left the table at that point; I was overcome with nausea and went outside in hopes that the fall air would make me feel better.

"My stomach was twisting now, as if there were something with claws inside me, trying to be born. The pain was horrible. I could not help remembering what I had read earlier that day, and how I had wished some part of me could be cut away. Right then, it was this writhing in my stomach—I wanted it cut away from me, surgically removed, taken out."

Izzy paused. He wiped his forehead on his sleeve. I noticed that I too was perspiring, although the draft from my rattling window was freezing. He looked into my eyes again, and again I had that nauseating sense that this story somehow implicated me.

"I don't know why I climbed into the ravine. I felt as if I were going to die, frankly, and I guess I thought that was as good a place to die as any. Anyway, I went down there. This was something I had never done alone before. Aaron had taken me to the ravine once when I was young, but I had been too frightened to go deep; I ran back to the top, and he laughed at me.

"Now, however, I climbed right down to the dark place at the bottom, where the shadows moved. From there I could see only one light from the city: it was the lit window of a house built into the side of the ravine. I remember staring at the window, as the shadows pulled around me, and the pain grew, until I had to close my eyes."

"Cut it away!" Izzy screamed. "Cut it away from me. I want to forget. Please, just let me sleep . . ."

The shadows circled and leapt. In a closet, in the room where the window was lit, a twisted doll smiled her half-smile. Izzy writhed on the floor of the ravine and cried bitter tears.

The seagulls called.

"Cut it away!"

Something stretched from his stomach to his throat, waking and stretching like a cat in the sunlight. Something with claws, slow lungs, and golden eyes. He felt the skin tear from his navel to his throat to accommodate the birth.

Izzy touched his chest, involuntarily, as he told me this. "Of course," he said, "when I stopped screaming, and stared at my stomach, there was nothing . . . my shirt hadn't even been torn."

He felt a great clawed arm extend through his solar plexus. It was tearing through him, this golden creature, but it was not tearing him apart. It was covered in liquid, as if it were just being born, and it was huge.

His ribs opened, yawned wide with a tearing noise, and then closed intact.

In the midst of his pain there was a moment of clarity. Izzy suddenly remembered Josh's answer at the dinner table, when his mother had asked again what Aaron's machine was designed to do.

Josh had spoken in a tiny quivering voice, full of fear and wonder.

"It'th for bringing puppieth to life."

Katie sat despondently at the window that was his door and stared at the sky. The relentless cloud showed no sign of diminishing. Across the city she could hear a siren, the sound strangely muffled. She waited.

There was another sound down in the shadows of the ravine, as if bones were cracking, and then a loud tearing. For the first time, Katie noticed that his eyes were gold. Not brown, but gold: the color of a lion's skin. Of a lion's eyes. Only one dye was poured into the substance that made the lion, and it is a calm, fathomless gold; to stare into the eyes of a lion is to swim in the presence of a cool and impenetrable soul whose windows are gold.

Then again, she could never be sure that he was not in fact canine, or human.

For the first time, Katie was frightened.

He picked her up as if she were a piece of thread and carried her up against the wall, where he pressed himself against her so that their hearts beat together, and she understood then that his heart beat far too slowly.

Desire can take fear and bend it until it is an ornament. Katie no longer knew why she was breathing so quickly, merely that she was. She put out her arms for the first time to touch him.

Every time he breathed, her face would cloud over with mist. There was another tearing noise, less horrible than the sound in the ravine, and she realized that he was tearing her gown. In strips. Strip by strip. Until she was clothed only in thin tatters of cloth.

And then, for the first time, he kissed her.

If a moment could be expanded to articulate its parts—and for the next year of her life she would try to do this in her mind—the sequence of that moment would unfold slowly like this: she felt his lips against hers, and closed her eyes to be for a moment almost alone in her happiness; and her happiness swelled into a brief delirium. And then she felt a hand between her legs, a cold, vicious hand, and then unspeakable agony as if something sharp had been driven through her, through her sex and up into her chest, and then the cold when her heart froze into white petals and then she screamed as the flower shattered under the hammer of his chest and she opened her eyes as wide as she could but they were still not wide enough to encompass those golden eyes. She realized, as she fell to the floor sobbing pitifully, that those eyes were mocking her. Laughing at her innocence, enjoying her pain. And then he was gone.

When she could at last lift herself from the tears and blood on the floor, she pulled herself still doubled over and crying to the night table, and as she stared at it she felt herself dying, and then dying again, and then dying again.

This time, he had left nothing.

2

TEMPLE

Nothing I have seen—in photographs or real life—ever cut me as sharply, deeply, instantaneously. Indeed, it seems plausible to me to divide my life into two parts, before I saw those photographs (I was twelve) and after, though it was several years before I understood fully what they were about. What good was served by seeing them? They were only photographs—of an event I had scarcely heard of and could do nothing to affect, of suffering I could hardly imagine and could do nothing to relieve. When I looked at those photographs, something broke. Some limit had been reached, and not only that of horror; I felt irrevocably grieved, wounded, but part of my feelings started to tighten; something went dead; something is still crying.

Susan Sontag

THEY WERE CAREFUL WITH IZZY FOR SOME TIME. He was not really an invalid; he still walked the same way, but he had changed. It was the incident with the machine, or so they thought. They needed a reason why young Izzy, once merely morose, had become alternately violent and sullen, had developed a laugh like an echo in a chimney.

Aaron was required to dismantle his device. There was no confrontation: his mother simply noted that the device had left Izzy half dead in the ravine and that he might wish to take up something else. Which he did. Weight lifting.

Izzy was handled gingerly. He received inappropriate sympathy. However vicious his behavior, he was forgiven. It was the shock, they said, the shock to the system.

Nobody ever corrected what he had learned in the library. There was nothing, of course, to correct: what he had read was true. Nobody, however, knew what he had read, and how it had changed him. Everything was attributed to the incident with the machine.

He began to laugh for the first time in his life. Openly, angrily, with grim condescension. It was not an unhappy time.

When Izzy finished grade six, it was expected that he would go to a private school. There were no academic standards to speak of in the public school system, and Izzy was thought to be scholarly. It came as a great surprise to everyone that he failed the entrance exams to every prestigious school in the province.

The precise content of his exam papers was considered private, so his parents never figured out what he had written. I know, however, that Izzy did not simply fail. He wrote such things that the teachers who marked the exams had disquieting dreams for years.

The truth was that he had no desire to be shut away with boys for the next seven years of his life. Adolescence was coming on, and he had some idea what he was in for. It would not be a good thing if the coming passion were forced to take some inward monastic path: he would pull himself inside out with longing. He wanted a public school.

Izzy ended up in a vast complex of blackened rufous brick, surrounded by miles of running track and football field, a monstrous symmetrical poorhouse of learning that, for all its faults, had one undeniable architectural virtue: it could never have been mistaken for anything but a high school in downtown Toronto.

He could not remember much of what occurred in the classroom. It seemed a form of ritual humiliation, perhaps, a kind of hell: those who could not teach condemned to spend eternity with those who could not learn.

Aaron was at St. Christopher's. It was the bluest of the private schools, strong on discipline and athletics, seven years subtly orchestrated so that young boys, mere potential upon arrival, would graduate with the reins of society in their hands, and with a talent, purely unconscious, for flicking their wrists to make the great horse canter without complaining.

They took boys with intelligence but a practical bent, boys with earthly greed. Izzy would not have been happy there. The students spent three hours a day on the playing fields. For two hours, they sat in a silent room in which study was supervised and enforced. The rest of the day was devoted to classes. There were no girls.

Aaron thrived. There was a large room with iron weights on pulleys and bars, and he was permitted to spend most of his three requisite hours in there, playing Sisyphus. Already large, he began to grow hard as well.

He had friends, weight room friends, and they found each other's rhythms comforting: the outward blow of air as the iron pushed upward, the soft thud as it met the ground, metal clicking against metal, pulleys creaking slowly. The room had the smell of a machine, a human machine. Izzy went to visit his brother once and was surprised how much it reminded him of Aaron's room at home when the great flywheel was still turning.

Josh wrote all the time now. Notes, he called them. The precise nature of his notes eluded the family until, by a cruel stroke of nature, they suddenly had both perfect access to him and none at all.

Josh hardly ever sang at home as he used to; instead he would hum softly to himself as he wrote. He still disappeared nightly, and when he returned he would disappear into his room to write. His room was full of paper, and their mother was no longer permitted to clean in there. She did not mind. She was comforted that Josh was telling stories, whether he sang them or committed them to paper. Why she was comforted, Izzy did not know; he had some notion of what these stories were, and it disturbed him profoundly.

"A new crisis was boiling in the family, and I was at the center. I was going to drag my family into a greater context, though all but my mother were unwilling to go. I was going to force a confrontation. I was going to turn thirteen.

"There was no question of Aaron's having a bar mitzvah. He had no more desire to learn Hebrew than he did Swahili or Romansh. Aaron's thirteenth birthday did, however, cause some tension at home. Though my father appeared faintly relieved, my mother was unusually distant as they brought out the cake and sang. Joshua sang beautifully, then retired to his room to make notes."

Izzy's thirteenth birthday would be more eventful.

"Abba did not know me, I thought, and this meant that he did not particularly care about my life. When he phoned I happened to pick up the receiver, and I went through the many motions I had perfected in the treatment of relatives, tracing the form of a casual conversation before passing the telephone over to my mother. This time, though, the ritual did not come to a clear conclusion. It did not seem that Abba was going to say, this time, 'Very nice talking to you, Isaac. Can I speak to your mother?' This time, he wanted to speak to me."

Would Isaac like to have dinner with him? Just the two of them? They would have dinner in his apartment. Abba would cook chicken.

Abba always called him Isaac.

Izzy was twelve. He could not have felt more peculiar than he did at the thought of having dinner, alone, in that illegible apartment, with his grandfather. What would he say? Or, perhaps more importantly, what would Abba say? Izzy had no doubt he had been called for a reason. His grandfather had reasons.

I clipped on a tie, without being told. I felt that a tie

would be appropriate. I felt, in fact, as if I were Josh off to the telling of a story.

My mother drove me. She was a precise driver. She drove with the understanding that there were breathing human bodies, barely protected, hurtling along beside her. Most people do not drive like this. It was always a calming sensation, driving with my mother; I was hardly ever as happy to be taken somewhere by another person.

I now know that the highway is a great mediator. There are collector lanes, devised to gather the will of the individual and pour it into a new mold: traffic, a predictable mass. If you drive, you stand to lose your soul. You stand to become part of the traffic pattern and subject to very simple laws. It was odd that I felt safe with her. In her determination to remain separate from the laws, she was in many ways like that car burning quietly by the side of the road.

We arrived at my grandfather's apartment building, and he let us up. It was generic, this apartment, but it contained such artifacts that it could never be mistaken for its thousand identical neighbors. All were white rooms, but this was a museum.

My mother met my grandfather at the front door and they kissed. I seem to remember they said nothing. I followed my grandfather in through the door, and my mother walked back to the elevator.

"So, Isaac. You are having a nice time at school?"

A difficult question to answer with any degree of honesty. I said, "It's okay."

"So. That's nice."

We sat in the living room, on hard chairs. Even the sofas were hard in Abba's apartment. Comfort was not an issue in the construction of his world.

"Are you reading books? Your mother tells me you read books."

"Yeah. I guess I do."

"That's nice."

We sat for a long moment in silence.

"In my family, I was the one who read books."

Abba walked over to the bookcase: old hardwood, set into the wall, filled with volumes of leather and yellow paper. He ran his hands over the curved spines. They were different from the books in our house, different materials, different dimensions; they did not sit on the shelf in the same way. "I used to read books."

Abba was examining my face. I in turn stared at the cut-glass decanter on the table in front of me. It was pregnant at the base and rose gracefully to a high neck, stopped with a glass stopper in the shape of an acorn. It had been blown in two layers, so that the outer layer, wine red, could be cut away in patterns to reveal a perfectly transparent layer beneath. I wondered what would happen if you filled the decanter with red wine: would the effect disappear?

It was sitting on an oblong serving tray of polished silver. On the wall was a diamond-shaped mirror, whose frame was also red glass, also cut away to reveal transparent patterns. They were inexpressibly foreign, these objects; they suggested a world that had died and could never be retrieved, a world of intrigue, in which clarity was obscured by a film of blood.

I wondered how Abba would break the silence.

"So maybe you'd like some chicken?"

He had set the dining table with the best silver. Just for the two of us. Perhaps this is all Abba had: the best silver. Silver with ovoid patterns at the end of each handle, eggs set in lace.

It felt peculiar to have all of this formality directed at me. I was, like most children, usually an incidental victim of ceremony, rarely its object.

Abba poured wine into the decanter. Thick sweet wine, which I loved then but which sickens me now. And it was true: where the glass was full of wine, the transparent pattern turned red and blended in.

He then poured me a small glass. I drank it quickly. So sweet as almost not to be wine, but I was happy with that. I did not yet like the taste of real wine. The thick liquid changed the temperature of my stomach. My cheeks flushed, and with them my mind. The room became warmer. A film of red crept across my eyes.

We seemed to be talking. While we ate chicken. I was keeping up my half, talking with Abba; I appeared to be saying the right things. But the room was becoming red; I was seeing all of these old dusty remnants through dim red glass.

I looked again at the decanter. As the wine emptied out, the pattern became apparent again. Later, when Katie lost her memory, I read books in hopes of curing her. Memory, the books said, is state-dependent. If you are drunk when you learn something, you will remember it again when you are drunk, but it will be difficult to remember when you are sober. That is why dreams are so difficult to conjure up when you are awake: your state has changed. What you learn when you sleep is almost impossible to call into the waking mind.

Abba was silent, again. He was looking at me. Still in silence, he rose and took a book down from the shelf. He opened it and placed it in front of me. "You can't read this, Isaac, can you?"

"No."

"It's Hebrew."

"I know."

"I spent the first half of my life reading Hebrew. Hebrew and Aramaic. Your Abba was a scholar. You would not know this from the way I lead my life, here, but I spent whole nights, whole nights until dawn, searching for the hidden keys to invisible locks, trying to find my way into the books. I would not eat for days, I was so concerned with the way in. Your Abba was like Hillel. You know this story? Your Abba wanted in, or to die of cold with his ear pressed to the window of the synagogue." He paused.

"It was admired, then, to be like that. If you could not comprehend the world . . . if you did not know anything about the vast world about you, but could read the most difficult books, you were counted wise. If you forgot to eat, that was not considered foolish. If it did not matter to you whether you lived or died . . ."

He closed the book, and put it back on the shelf. "History proved me a fool. If you do not care whether you live or die, they will take your life. All of my friends are dead—all of them scholars. They died so young. They were murdered, you see, because all they knew how to do was read. I came here, to Canada, and tried to become a member of this world. Your mother did not learn Hebrew. I wanted her to know how to live. I wanted her to care whether she lived or died."

I was embarassed to be hearing this. My grandfather had never said anything before; we all assumed he had nothing to say. What he was saying, now, was that he too was a stranger, and that his strangeness had made him silent. What he saw in me was not a generic grandson, but an ally.

"You read books, Isaac. A few years ago I would have thought that was a bad thing, that you were in danger of becoming like me, that you would become like the sheep. The sheep is a good animal, one of God's animals, but he does not complain as he waits for the slaughter, and this has sullied his name in the eyes of the butchers. I thought you would become like this."

He paused.

"And perhaps you will. Nevertheless, I have changed my mind."

Abba looked out the window at the suburban landscape: lowrises, gray and similar; one manicured lawn spreading out to the horizon.

"There is no place for me here. And my grandson is like me. He is. I can see that." He turned back towards me. "The more you try to become a good citizen of this world, Isaac, the less you will have to say."

His eyes, the whites yellowing with age, had always seemed tired; now they were alive, grieving and wild.

"I don't know what you read, Isaac, but I know why you are reading. You can see your city for what it is—a shameful place. Look at it. Two million people, and it means nothing. And so you are trying to escape. But where will you go, Isaac? Where will you go?"

He tapped a long finger against the bookshelf. "There is some thing to be read in these books. There is. I never said so before, because I did not want you to be like me. I thought it was wrong to want to die, frozen, with your ear pressed against the glass. But I have changed my mind."

His voice became hard. He was issuing a command. "You're my grandson. You're going to be thirteen. I want you to learn Hebrew."

I remained silent in the car on the way home. It did not feel right. I should have been happy; Abba had opened himself up to me, had opened an old world and invited me in; an ancient responsibility had been placed on my shoulders.

I would nominally accept the task. I would learn Hebrew and be called. But I felt like a criminal, a skulking thief—I knew there was a part of me, a golden predator with slow warm breath, that had separated from my conscious will, that I no longer owned. It would do what it would do. Even now, for all I knew, I was no longer innocent.

Nor would I be innocent, whatever I felt then. My decision to have a bar mitzvah changed everything, subtly. Ours was a silent family; the pressure and heat moved well beneath the surface of the earth. But there was movement. Something volcanic had been boiling quietly for years. My decision caused, I believe, the first visible cracks to appear.

*   *   *

"The last time I was in my mother's library was some years ago," Izzy said. "I didn't go to her apartment very often, and when I did I would hide in the library, as I did when I was young.

"Now that the family was over, the books had become objects of contention. Who owned which book suddenly mattered, and my mother was afraid to let a book out of the house for fear it would end up in the library of my father. As if they could own these books. Or prevent someone else from owning my childhood.

"She had preserved the order of the books. There was an entire shelf devoted to dinosaurs. My infatuation with dinosaurs was not ordinary, although many boys shared it to a lesser degree. I could pronounce 'paleontologist' in grade two, because that was what I was going to be.

"She still had the books they used to teach me Hebrew. There, on the shelf above dinosaurs. Books with pictures of happy children in skullcaps at summer camp, cloying and bland; children who did not exist.

"Some fell for it, I suppose: those insipid characters designed to instill in us a sense of comfort. Judaism is not dangerous; it's fun—good clean fun—a healthy alternative to Boy Scouts. You can be a good Jew, if you just settle into a middling world of nice.

"Was this what Abba had in mind? I could not imagine anyone going without food for one of these books.

"A mentor some years after my bar mitzvah, Professor Abraham Gold, would object to the word 'nice' on the grounds that it was weakness made language, that it expressed no solid stance. Thumbing through these books, I had to disagree. 'Nice' is one of the most potent words in the English language. It levels meaning. Erodes dignity. Prevents attainment. It is the barrier between a society and heroism. If you acquiesce and become nice, you are lost.

"Abraham was a revolutionary. Bar Kokhba was a dangerous man. These were terrifying people; they bore the burden of a terrifying faith. I had to go elsewhere to find out what Abba had spoken about. In other books, books my parents never bought, I read about the young Rabbi Akiba, how he spent all night one Passover with two fellow rabbis contemplating the Chariot in Ezekiel; God's body; his physical nature. A dangerous night, contemplating the imponderable. By morning the other two rabbis had lost their faith, and with it everything, the rational world; they were mad, slavering, singing, no longer teachers, no longer men, diseased bodies, the soul wrung right out. Rabbi Akiba stepped into the strong morning sun, a wise man.

"In one book there was a picture of Akiba ben Joseph. 'One of the very famous rabbis in Jewish history.' A smiling, kind, fond old fool. Santa Claus. As sweet a man as ever looked into the abyss.

"One thing I do not regret. That was my decision, early in life, that I would be anything but nice."

At breakfast, the day after I had met with Abba, I announced my decision. I was twelve; I wanted to learn Hebrew, or at least enough to waddle through an ancient ceremony; I was going to have a bar mitzvah.

When I announced this, my father brought his index

finger down upon the table. I knew immediately that there was another member of my family I would have to get to know if I were to understand my predicament.

My father had always been peripheral, functional, a constant. I had never felt the need to know what kind of wires and pipes lay beneath the surface of the walls in our house—I felt I knew those walls sufficiently well—and I was satisfied with how well I knew my father. Until that moment.

His finger hammered against the wood to produce such a sound that the whole family was immediately quiet. It was as if he had brought his fist down. My mother looked away. Who was this man, I began to think, who could confine his violence to a single finger, with this kind of result?

I saw for the first time that there was immense control in my father. He controlled many things, beginning with himself. But he did not control my mother. And, with my wish to learn Hebrew, he was worried that he was losing me as well.

Who was he? I was surprised to recognize that, up until now, I had not really wanted to know. But now, with the hammer fall of a finger, I was made to see that he was an integral piece in my initial puzzle: if I were to understand my mother, it was in opposition to him. She was figure; he was ground. There was something perverse about this. In the old world my mother would have been the landscape.

It was expected, simply expected, that I would not have a bar mitzvah. I had done violence to expectations.

Aaron sneered.

*   *   *

As I learned Hebrew, I began to steal. The Hebrew lessons were given on Saturday mornings in the basement of Blessed Palm, and in the afternoons I would take the subway downtown and lift things from the stores.

Blessed Palm is an unlikely synagogue. In North America, the Jewish faith is divided roughly into three degrees of worship: Orthodox, Conservative, and Reform. The Reform movement is an attempt to determine the degree to which the modern Jew can assimilate without becoming, say, Christian. Blessed Palm is perhaps the most extreme experiment in this regard: situated in the middle of the wealthiest Jewish neighborhood, it caters to professionals who do not wish to seem too conspicuous in their faith. Architecturally, it is a mercurial masterpiece. Stockbrokers have noted how the public spaces have the same comforting feeling as the trading floor; lawyers feel as if they are in a courtroom; politicians find the atmosphere approaches the clean blue taste of parliament. Blessed Palm is a professional synagogue.

Hebrew was taught by Misha. He had hair down to his waist and played a big acoustic guitar, a Martin Dreadnought; word had it he was in line to inherit an empire of dry goods. Between conjugations, Misha would pick up the guitar and sing protest songs. Sometimes he would chair a discussion. We would discuss ethics, mostly: "Is it possible to be a good Jew, and yet cheat your neighbor in business?" The answer to this one was a resounding no.

"Can you be a good Jew, and have sexual relations before marriage?" The girls, aged twelve, were surprisingly uncertain on this one, although the boys almost unanimously agreed that their sexual behavior was independent of their goodness as Jews. Misha, strumming A minor, intervened with a compact piece of universal wisdom: "The only thing that matters, in sexual relations, is that you don't hurt anyone, and you don't let anyone hurt you."

I still ponder this aphorism. I have considerably less respect for the Mishas of the world than I did at that time, and even then I was wary, but I think often about that advice. I have decided that it is true: the only thing that matters is that no one get hurt. Of course, I have never witnessed sexual relations in which nobody got hurt.

And so I learned Hebrew, liberally sweetened with folk music, and thieved in the afternoons.

I cannot tell you much about Hebrew, the language. It was generally acknowledged at Blessed Palm that it was sufficient to learn how to pronounce the bar mitzvah passage: comprehension was asking too much of the tender young mind. This attitude was perhaps inherited from the public school system. It is mandatory to study French for almost a decade in the province of Ontario, and yet you are not required to learn French. I have never, in fact, met anyone who learned French in the classrooms of Ontario.

I pronounced Hebrew fluently. I can say things, in this incomprehensible language, with real feeling. I was to pronounce my passage with such conviction that it would bring tears to the eyes of my bar mitzvah audience (almost none of whom understood Hebrew). Misha was a good teacher.

I, on the other hand, made Misha nervous. Once,

when he was singing a song about the proletariat, I asked him how much his guitar cost.

"It's . . . well, it's a good guitar."

"But how much did it cost?"

"You have to understand, Izzy, that this was . . . a good year for Martin guitars. The best. So . . . it was expensive."

"How much?"

He told me. As he finished his song, a very moving piece about a miner's wife who was starving because her husband was coughing up his lungs, a song that ended with a generalized plea to level the bitterness of inequality, I noticed that Misha played with less fervor than usual: his big Martin guitar was not making a very big noise. It sounded as if it wanted to disappear.

I do not mean to imply that Misha was not a good Jew, simply that I made him nervous.

I stole mostly from the large department stores, because they were easiest. I was so small I escaped notice. I started by stealing tiny objects, anything that could be cupped in my palm, but I grew adventurous in my success. The largest item I ever stole, without any help from the Friends, was a television. I simply walked out the front door with it. Nobody would have the audacity to carry a large television out the front door without paying for it. So they thought. In fact, the security guard offered to help me down the stairs with it.

One the street, a man asked me if I could spare a quarter. I gave him the television. I did not have a quarter.

The Friends changed all of this. Not just the scale,

but the quality of the operation. Televisions, though expensive, are worthless. Together, we learned how to steal items of value.

Though Josh seemed to have no sense that I had entered his secret life as a spectator, I had a strong sense that he had entered mine. He knew I was a thief. There was no judgment in his look, but the distance had multiplied between us.

Aaron neither knew nor cared. He had made headway in his personal life: one Saturday, he and the weight room boys had succeeded in lifting a tractor-trailer and placing it in a neighbor's back garden. The headmaster at St. Christopher's had been notified, and he had punished them with a smile; it was the sort of misdemeanor that was encouraged in that environment, like skipping classes to practice rowing. Aaron's transgressions seemed less profound than mine: I was the one who was going against my nature, who had split and attacked himself like a spider eating its young.

Misha was aware of my difference from the rest of his students. They spent as much on clothes as he did on guitars; I spent money on almost nothing. Sometimes I would arrive at Hebrew class with a small, expensive object, which I would play with as we discussed difficult questions, but it was always an object I had stolen.

I said very little, and even then only when I had something particularly disturbing to say. I was not well liked by the other students. They were not afraid of me, nor scandalized; they simply did not like me very much. At Blessed Palm, you were either in or out. Either you went to a summer camp where they served the

86

finest lox, or you did not. If not, time was not wasted peering into your idiosyncrasies; you were ignored. I did not like them, either.

Misha was certainly not fond of me, but he could not ignore me. Much of Misha's life had been spent seeking—not very efficiently, but seeking nevertheless. The guitar and the hair were symbols of complacency; they were the trappings of dogma. They said: I have found it; I do not have to seek further. I knew even less than Misha, but he saw in me what he thought he had conquered in himself: homelessness. I was a reminder that he had come to rest, not at the end of his quest, but in the most comfortable chair he could find.

The students adored Misha. Always in the front of their minds, despite his gentle ways, was that he stood to inherit a fortune in dry goods. Besides, his dull ethical proddings made them feel good. They were, almost uniformly, an intelligent group, and there was something uneasy in the way their lives smoothly slid forward. They wanted answers, quickly, to some difficult questions. Misha had all the answers.

I wanted to see some of the girls naked. That was the closest I could come to expressing a strong interest in this group.

The Friends were altogether different. Woolly and dangerous, I called them out of the cracks and sewers of adolescence. I conjured them. They were my familiars.

Campbell was simply there, one day, like a black cat, small and careful. His hair was so dark as to be almost blue; he cut it himself with paper scissors and Dickensian results. Campbell was smart. He had seen me reading. He had read the books I read, and more besides. He arrived at my side and stayed there, and like a black cat, he would not let on whether he was my pet or I was his.

Campbell was quiet at first. He had approached me; therefore, in that early friendship, I was more powerful than he was. I expressly needed nobody, and at best suffered an acquaintance. Campbell obviously saw something in me.

I should have watched him. But I was flattered, so I let him stay.

Campbell was the first of the Friends. How we acquired that name I do not remember, but we used the term as if it had quotation marks. We were trying to drain any sentiment out of the word—we were virtually opposed to sentiment—but looking back I wonder if we were not in fact being truly sarcastic: we called each other Friends as you might call a basketball player Shorty.

I taught Campbell how to steal. He expressed no surprise when I told him this is what I intended to do. If I stole, he would steal as well. After all, we read the same books.

It was interesting to watch Campbell learn. For the first week, the apprenticeship, he watched me aggressively, with hunger, until he knew everything about theft that I knew. By the second week, he had bettered my technique in every way.

We developed complex strategies, diversionary tactics. Campbell stood lookout, and when he saw that I was attracting undue attention, he would create an alternative spectacle. These dramas were sometimes so appealing in their own right that I would stop, in midtheft, to watch Campbell's antics. Often this would nullify the effect of the diversion: by the time the tactic was complete, I was no further along in the process of the theft, and Campbell would have to create some new disturbance. The first time this happened, he became angry until I suggested, smiling, that he didn't seem to have the stomach for a challenge. He did not become angry again.

Campbell began to introduce me to a new kind of theft. He had the uncanny ability to find objects that had been left in dark places for so long that they had been forgotten: heirlooms in attics, old silver in locked drawers, even small caches buried in gardens. We would find our way into houses, at night, and take things that nobody would ever miss, because it was forgotten that they were there.

Once I asked Campbell about this: how, if the families who owned these things could not remember that they owned them, did he know about them? It was not trial and error: Campbell would always take me directly to the object of our theft, without hesitation. He never properly answered, but sometimes, as if in response, he would waver in my sight, become less solid: the light would shine through him and I would feel a cold wind against my neck as if I were in the presence of the dead.

Once, in a locked basement, we found an old children's toy, a stuffed lion almost a century old. It lay in an oaken toy chest, and beneath it was a small photograph in faded sepia. When I picked up the photo, wondering if it would give some clue to the history of this pathetic toy, I again had this deathly touch on my neck.

It was a picture of Campbell.

I was sure of it; it was a picture of Campbell's face, though many years younger, perhaps six years old. I looked up, to compare his face beside me with the photograph in sepia, but he was gone.

That night, when I found my way back to my room with the stuffed lion hidden beneath my shirt, there was a moment when the toy seemed to grow warm, and then a spike of terrible pain. When I removed my shirt, I found four small puncture marks in the skin of my stomach, where the lion's paw had rested against me.

"I should have watched Campbell as carefully as he watched me." Izzy sat for a moment, contemplating this.

"I did not realize, until too late, that he bore a grudge for the slightest perceived humiliation, that he felt I had humiliated him more than once, and that he had an elaborate concept of revenge.

"Campbell, almost immediately after this brief initiation, began to plan the most intricate crime."

Though I tried to remain anonymous at school, it was hard not to notice the only student who seemed to care less about the classroom than I did: a girl named Margaret.

Margaret seemed to spend most of her time by the school gate, smoking with her friends. She too was above learning, but for different reasons: she had a social itinerary more complex than calculus. School for her was a place to run with the girls. This school in particular was well suited to this activity, because so little time had to be devoted to anything else. For girls like Margaret, smoking was not a vice, but an attribute to be acquired at a certain age with one's first yellow cashmere.

When I took up cigarettes, it was with an entirely different aim. I smoked to fill my clothes with the scent of age, the stale accumulation of late nights. My uniform was parodic: mostly bits and pieces from various private school uniforms, poorly matched, but essentially conservative in style.

I smoked so that I would have something to hold in my hand at four in the morning when I could not afford another cup of coffee and my hand shook too much to hold one without spilling even if I could. This was absurd: I was still so small that my head barely rose above the coffee counter. I would light one cigarette off the other, and would breathe pure air only at meals or when I slept.

Where we acquired the rest of the Friends I can barely remember. I say that I conjured them, but sometimes I think they just arrived, on schedule, to fill the parts Campbell wrote for them. Ainsley, Lewis, Cran.

Ainsley was the tallest, taller than my brother Aaron. He had limp and greasy curls, which he wore tied in the back. He lived, slept, and breathed in a black tuxedo jacket, which was too short in the arms and gave him the look of a lean gorilla. Ainsley was slow, in the way tall people can be, lazy and bent, but he was wicked; if an idea met with his approval, an evil grin would slowly spread across his face like an oil slick on water.

Lewis never spoke. He was like the wind in a blind alley: silent and stale, rustling occasionally, capable of gusting in a way that made your back crawl. Moments of quick, ruthless action were his forte, and they were sometimes required.

Cran, who came with Lewis, never stopped speaking. He was a couple of years older, and drove a car. When called upon to drive quickly, Cran would speak at double tempo, as if his chatter were necessary fuel. He was always moving, clenching and unclenching his muscles, staying limber.

The five of us together were impressive.

Margaret, at least, thought as much. The Friends would meet at irregular hours in the most remote stairwell at school, and somehow Margaret managed to be there more often than not, just passing through. She would look at us wryly, as if she disapproved, but she would stand and talk to us until we left.

For weeks, she hovered like this on the periphery, free of us, like a seagull riding the air. We affected indifference, but we would talk with her.

After a while, however, as my involvement with the Friends became increasingly complex, I found that something was happening in my attitude towards this girl. My breath was beginning to quicken in her presence, in a way that was new and unexpected. It was a new kind of desire. It was the need that sliding men have, a sexual need, for someone good.

She had no idea what it was we did, as Friends. Had she known explicitly from the start, what happened between us might never have begun; but she had no concrete notion back then, merely a sense that I was dangerous, that I might speed up her life like a motorcycle or a fall from a cliff.

My father made tentative efforts to know me. My decision was of interest to him. Why had I decided to become, even nominally, Jewish? I thought he might benefit as a public figure from evidence of piety in his family, but I was wrong. It is an advantage, in the public life of the city, to be religious in a muted, sensible way. It is an advantage to have beliefs, as long as they do not influence policy; beliefs are a character trait, and speak well of a man. Certain beliefs, however, are thought neither muted nor sensible. Judaism, for instance, while politely tolerated, is best confined to medicine, law, and the entertainment industries.

My apparent piety, as long as it never got out of hand, would only embarrass my father marginally if he remained at his present station in life, but it would put a ceiling on his ambitions. If he ever entertained the desire to become a national figure, or to encourage Aaron in that direction, my tendency to embrace odd rituals would be positively menacing.

It was only later, when I discovered something of my father's reasons in life, that I regretted my treasonous activities. I never realized how hard he had fought for simply respectability, for the right not to be excluded from the most basic institutions. His desire for a clean, homogeneous city, in which he might become a full member if he sufficiently erased his personal history, was not snobbery, nor was it greed: it was a response to a brand of hatred whose subtlety and virulence I had never experienced except in books, and certainly never associated with Toronto.

It took a great deal to get my father interested in a person. I have no doubt that he had always loved me, in that silent architectural way that constitutes the family bond, but I am sure he was never interested in me until now. My father was sad that I had not inherited his life's project, and it was because of this sadness that he now wanted to know me.

"You like Hebrew?" he asked me.

"It's okay."

"I took Hebrew for seven years."

This should not have been a surprise, but it was.

"Don't remember a thing. Hated it."

This struck him as perhaps a severe thing to say, and it was; it certainly shut me up, so he tried a softer approach.

"But then, you read a lot of books. I guess a new language is pretty interesting." I think even he was stunned by the intellectual level of this comment; my father was an intelligent man.

"Gives you a lot more books to read," I said, helpfully.

"Well," he said.

One afternoon, in the desperation of boredom, I tore Margaret's underwear in the stairwell.

She had appeared, magically, when the Friends arrived, and remained there with me when they disappeared. Why I wanted to put my fingers up her then and there I don't know; I suppose I wanted to be judged, and the way to ensure judgment is to push the private into the public.

There is a critical momentum in the act of seduction, a speed that once achieved cannot be withstood. It leaves both parties gasping, glazed, and can precipitate acts uncontemplated—incapable of being contemplated at the pace of an ordinary day. I felt myself gaining speed in the bratty innocence of Margaret's sphere, whirling about her cotton dress like an electron, putting my hands on her tight skin.

The stairwell wound above us in dizzying spirals, a cast-iron strand of DNA, and framed us in its crazy focus, two children breathing drugged air and whirling at the base.

"Izzy, I don't know . . ."

Does anybody know, Margaret? You came here to talk to me, and now we're alone, the dancing lead bobs on the end of the helical spring, your breath so urgent and insistent betrays you.

"I don't *know*," she insisted, but she would find out, and if knowledge was a goal, then experimentation had its place. I put my hand up her back, shivering, then down and pulled and something, some flimsy piece of cotton, came away in my fingers. Raptor, I thought: eagles tear what they touch.

"You've torn my underwear." But it was not an accusation so much as a statement of wonder; and I think she even may have smiled, a frightened smile.

Margaret was wet there, and I felt the weight of my

95

transgression: to know a girl for some time and never before feel that wet, though you know she is a girl and must sometimes be wet; the personal experience, the particularity of the softness changes the time you have known her, irrevocably. There was no going back. What my hand was doing was like a word said: it would never be unsaid. It had become a fact.

"Izzy . . ." And as she said my name she leaned into me as if she wanted to push me out of the way but wanted even more that I not move, and I noticed for the first time that she was crying.

Campbell was secretive. "I have found something tremendously valuable," he said. "Something we want."

He was planning the most ambitious theft yet.

"My father changed after the rift. He wanted my mother out of his life, there is no doubt about that, but even the finest engineer sometimes removes a wall and finds that the structure has shifted beyond calculation: that there are cracks in the room upstairs, that a steel bearing will roll on the floors. My father inadvertently removed a great structural wall, and found himself listing.

"He became milder, almost friendly, and I remarked on this because the same thing happened to me.

"There is nothing like a degree of loneliness to create good manners; starving men learn quickly to say please. I saw him for the first time some years after the rupture, and he tried to entertain me as if I were a young man he had just met at the office. A new recruit. As his son I had always been foreign to him, so I suppose he approached me in this new way in hopes of winning me as a friend. I am not sure we shall ever be friends. I tried not to take sides in the rift, but I found myself straddling a chasm, and I had to jump. I am somewhere closer to my mother, though I am far even from her."

Izzy paused.

"I have spent a long time wondering about permanence: whether the soul can sustain irreparable damage, and how this might limit the notion of free will. Whether the psychologists are correct or not—and I am sure they are mostly not—we do carry our families with us, until death; and if our families are broken we carry the breakage in our soul."

It is not hard to understand how important the Friends became to me. There must be an inner circle, a place of holiness and trust, and with my parents weakening I had to turn somewhere else. Women ought to have become that place in my life—I wanted that from the start—but I found my dealings with them complicated by horrible passions.

My relations with Margaret were mostly silent and necessary, like a breath drawn in pain; I would clutch at her clothes within seconds of meeting her and we would apply ourselves to each other like vampires.

She hated this. I knew from the start that she hated her need for me, because it drew her into an increasingly humiliating situation. She wanted me to talk to her, to know her, to find her out, but I could never do this. I convinced myself that I simply did not want to, but I know now that it had something to do with the books I had read in the library: I wanted no part of anything that I might some day lose. More than this: I could imagine, vividly, the circumstances in which she might be torn from me. I had dreams of jackboots, long knives, and unspeakable decisions.

I kept Margaret at a distance, except that I would run my hands beneath her dress and tear at her mouth with mine; she tolerated this only because she hoped, with the kind of absurd hope that perhaps characterizes our species, that I would change. I never let her know that I needed her in any way other than this: my need was insistent and temporary; it disappeared with my lust.

I was reducing her. She was becoming an object of convenience. Margaret was becoming my slave.

The Friends I needed in a different way. A doctor once explained to me, in terms I still don't understand, that the ego requires a floor: perhaps what he was pointing at was how we sink into terror when trust dissolves. At any rate, I needed to trust these shadows, because they provided me with community, a sense of place, a floor.

Campbell in particular I came to need the more I tested him, the more he won my admiration. Campbell always came through. You could throw a curve at him, and he would catch it almost without moving.

The plans for the new crime were being drawn around me. It was exciting. The notion of invading a private place sparked a particular glow: invasion of the most private is the goal of a whole category of desires. My attachment to Margaret glowed, for instance, in this way.

Campbell and I took to walking at night, even when

we were not stealing. He would put a ladder to my window, and we would elope like lovers. All solid things take on breath during the night—they become less substantial and more alive, mortal and ghostly. Campbell seemed a piece of this darkness; it gave him strength. I grew to understand Aaron's experiments, or at least the impulse behind them; in my own way, as I grew closer to Campbell, I grew strangely convinced of the notion that the dead could be brought to life.

There is no doubt that, in the day, ours is a city of dying flesh. Toronto is a bank, really, and men go the way of paper bills; they become dim, wrinkled, soft with age, and are retired from circulation. Yet even a bank has mystery at night.

We would go out when the streets were wet and move through the city like amphibians. We would stand in the wind between the towers and laugh like owners. We would spend, and buy, and around us the city would breathe. Campbell was no longer my apprentice—he was planning a crime of his own—and I needed him as I would never need another boy.

Everything is confused at that age: friendship hurts more than love.

I had my entire bar mitzvah portion memorized. Misha had warned us not to memorize, because we would find ourselves at the altar reeling off the text without following the written words. Then, if we had a sudden lapse of memory, we would be utterly lost.

Simply to annoy him, I memorized the entire passage, both forwards and backwards. Sometimes, when he was getting on my nerves, I would recite it in reverse. I could do that with words: they floated in front of my mind like objects, and I could read them any which way.

I did not have to sing my portion, as they did in more rigorous synagogues, but there were a couple of prayers I was required to chant. I was surprised to find the melodies familiar. Later, I realized that they were among the songs Josh hummed beneath his breath at the dinner table.

Hebrew lessons were now worse than useless. The most I could hope to do, now that I had my portion memorized, was to begin to understand it. I had no desire to do this.

I took to arriving five minutes before the end of the class. I would go to the synagogue at the right time, but instead of descending into the basement where Misha held court, I would explore.

It was not an ordinary building. Though, as I have said, it was capable of being all things to all people, this was a characteristic only of the public spaces; the synagogue also had a hidden agenda, which could not be designed out of it despite the best intentions of the modernizing architect. Ordinary buildings, at least in Toronto, were made in such a way as to lead nowhere at all; the lobby, the office, and the washroom were each at the same stage in the ritual of the plan. The synagogue, however, had some ancient progression printed like memory in the shape of its floor, and it led somewhere. It took you, if you explored, into increasingly secret cavities: rooms into which only the initiated were allowed, then those into which nobody could go without naked fear.

I sense, sometimes, that the building was a conscious mind. There were rooms within rooms, each taking up more space than the room in which it was contained, each impossibly large. I was particularly enamored of the Great Chapel.

There was a dome over the altar. It had been painted blue, so that it fooled the eye: it looked like a piece of receding sky. A window.

So young that I could barely read, I remember asking my mother which was the rabbi—she had taken us to a Yom Kippur service, despite my father's objections. She pointed vaguely at the front of the chapel, and I thought she was pointing at the tiny piece of the sky. Since at that time I had conflated the ideas "rabbi" and "God," I felt sure that this blue sky, so elegantly captured by an architectural frame, was God incarnate: that He was overlooking the ceremony like a mild blue eye. It was years before I was disabused of this notion. My discovery that the rabbi was in fact not God at all, but the little man standing at the lectern, was something of a watershed in my conception of the world.

Once, while skipping off from Hebrew, I climbed the catwalks at the top of the Great Chapel—they had been installed to facilitate the changing of light bulbs—and I found myself standing beside the blue painted dome. God, as I then knew him, was an arc of cracking plaster, patched in places, painted a dull robin's egg blue.

I looked down over the empty seats, which would in a few weeks be filled with distant relatives. I had the urge to set myself on fire, to dive from my place at the dome and fly burning into the memory of the floor.

Misha entered the chapel. He had dismissed the class early. He didn't see me, standing where I was: an angel beneath the darkened ceiling.

I whispered: "Misha."

He turned, terrified, trying to divine the source of the voice.

"Misha."

He was white now, turning, his head moving in a peculiar jerking arch.

"Misha.

"Misha.

"Misha."

"There is no place for blasphemy in my life," said Izzy, unconvinced. "It makes no sense for me to blaspheme."

He examined his fingernails, which were black with filth as if he had been scraping in a garden.

"It was Margaret who wanted to see the synagogue."

Margaret would challenge me, as if she were in competition. I now realize that she was competing not with me but with Campbell and the Friends; she refused to be marginal, unnecessary, the girl, and she began to associate this condition with being good. She had a way of tipping her head back and to the side, dismissively, as she suggested something we might do: it was a challenge, and to ignore it would be cowardice.

This was her way of suggesting that I might bring her with me to a Saturday morning class: "Why don't you take me with you. Perhaps I'd like to learn Hebrew."

I did not take her to Misha's class. She was too much

of another place, even more alien there than I was, with her long athletic body and thin features, as if she had been drawn with a sharp pen. She carried herself with an arrogant reserve that had nothing to do with the girls in that class, who were voluble and raucous; Margaret was contained.

We slipped immediately into the Great Chapel, and I suggested, in a manner similar to one of her challenges, that we climb up on the catwalks. I knew that she, too, was afraid of falling.

Hence when we at last set foot on the solid concrete space beneath the blue dome, we were both in that breathless state that comes from mocking fear; we had both been pretending that there was something beneath us more solid than that volume of air; we had both fallen in our minds a hundred times, and cried out silently with every step.

She clutched me as we stepped off the catwalk and forced her mouth to mine, but I knew that it was not purely amorous, this. She wanted to drive that fear out of her body with something more terrible: desecration. She wanted to turn the fear until it looked like something else: will, hunger, a pushing against and taking in. She took the hair at the back of my head in her fist, held her fist to the back of my neck like a knot of blood, and pushed her tongue into my mouth.

We were bruising each other; the challenge of the catwalk had united us in fever; I could feel the points where her fingers bit into my back go red, and I again tore her clothing, so that she was half uncovered beneath the blue painted eye of the dome.

As she pulled me to the floor, so that we were out of

sight of the chapel below, we both heard the great door in the far wall open and then close with a hydraulic hiss. Margaret gave me that look again, mocking, challenging me to continue despite our unwitting audience, testing me. I pulled her dress up about her shoulders.

He began to sing. Whoever had entered the chapel was now at the altar, singing a prayer in a young soprano voice—a voice I would have known anywhere, so often had I heard it filtering through the walls of our house. Margaret held my mouth to her breast, and I bit her.

My stomach felt small and hard. I was supposed to sing at my bar mitzvah, and this was the voice I was supposed to have—a voice of smoke and honey, capable of calling terrible glory from the indifferent sky—but I knew that mine was cracking with cold desire for Margaret, cracking in the freeze-and-thaw cycle of my capricious need, like a wintering road.

It was increasingly apparent that Margaret was suffering, though she was too proud to say so. I never did speak to her, though she continued to wait; I had nothing to say to her. She remained with me only because she was still hoping that I would discover something in her that I could respect and want to know; I could have told her that there was no hope of this.

Certainly, she had a hook in her breath, like mine, and could ache for the wordless and forbidden, but it was not what she wanted. It was what she suffered, in her foolish hope that I might change.

She was beginning to develop that look. Silent blame,

suffering and expectation. It made me sick, but I continued to have her; as long as she was there, I would not be the one to turn away.

My midnight walks with Campbell were becoming more ambitious. Years later, when I told Katie about these evenings, she became silent and thoughtful. I think she saw more significance in my relationship with Campbell than I ever did.

"He was wrapping you up," she finally said. "Winding threads about you. People can only do that to other people at night."

It was true that he was pulling me in. I was so accustomed to my lonely strength that I would not admit to myself it was being eroded, until it was much too late.

Campbell was supposed to be my inferior; I was supposed to be teaching him. Campbell, however, had never wanted to be the student. He was determined to teach me something before he left. He watched me with Margaret and he saw what I did: he knew that I did not properly suffer. Campbell would teach me.

Katie would make much of this period of my life. She said there were times in everybody's life, events, which you could point to: they were the times when the set design fell into place, when the stage took its essential form, when the obstacles were placed on the way to the wings. If you identified these points properly, then you had the person in focus. You knew why they did what they did. There could be more than one such event, just as a play can change scenery between acts, but this business with Campbell was the most recent in my life, the one that exerted the greatest force on my immediate circumstances.

It was important to Katie to understand this moment in my life. It was important, because my scenery would increasingly close upon her: we became subplots—and then the main narrative—of the same play.

My last day with Margaret ended in words. The silence that had defined our shaking hands was challenged, and could no longer bind us.

I had known her, by then, for a long time. I had watched her change, and she me; we ought to have had the common interest in each other that time brings, the watching of life unfolding. But passion can do something abortive to the memory if you're not careful; months of careful and subtle change can be forgotten in the immediacy of want. We were not careful. *I* was not careful.

We were to meet that evening in the middle of an aluminum sculpture. It was known as St. Alcan by the students at the university, since it had been erected in the center of the Catholic college.

If you stood inside this sculpture, you could not be seen from most angles. Occasionally somebody might walk by an opening and wonder, but that was a risk that only heightened the pleasure. I had proposed that we meet there, and Margaret had tentatively agreed. St. Alcan was composed of bright aluminum slabs, which met in a tall apex and surrounded a tiny area in which two people could stand with ease. This is where I stood, waiting for her.

I think back often about the points of the rupture. The time when what is said is too strong ever to be rescinded, when what is done is too dire ever to be forgiven. These points are intimately connected to the notion of irreparable psychic damage: they are the exterior equivalents, and they have corresponding interior repercussions. Once you have heard somebody cry in a certain way, you cannot separate from them without violence.

Margaret stood passively at the opening to the statue.

"Come inside," I whispered.

"No. You come out here."

I stepped out from behind the veil of white metal, and stood inches away from her. She looked at me with eyes I had seen before, though I did not recognize them now.

"Aren't you going to touch me?"

I looked about. We were fully in public. Though the square in which the statue stood was isolated, and it was now dark, anybody could walk through at any time. I lifted her skirt and pushed my hand between her angry legs.

She hung about my neck and between sharply drawn gasps, said: "I hate you."

And she began to claw at my neck, gasping like a trapped animal. She said other things, too, as she pushed herself up and down against me as if trying to escape. I knew the sensation she was after: it was a certain thrill of release, a fever of freedom, the kind the fox has when it leaves a leg behind in the trap.

I didn't reply to anything she said. The fear of being

caught had worked me into a criminal lust, and I was incapable of guilt.

Her breath came like a collapsing lung. "You only like to hear me breathe like this because you think it's you who makes my breath sound this way . . ."

And she cried, a tremor of pain it seemed. A thin student entered the quadrangle, stared at us in a moment of comprehension and shock, slipped away.

"I have a name, Izzy . . ."

My words make sense to me now like the thick rose-colored lines on a plan; the lines that indicate where the cut was made, where the wall was cut at knee-level to open up the structure of the building, the sequence of rooms. Where the wall was cut. I said, "Margaret," and even in pronouncing her name, it was as if I were making a clinical incision, highly clinical and abstract, all for the sake of a drawing. "Margaret . . ."

And she cried out again, this time unmistakably. It was the pleasure of rending, the bleeding freedom from the trap, the shuddering fact of divorce.

In the morning, Margaret's father phoned my mother. I knew it was him on the phone—I answered—so I remained on the line, listening quietly.

His daughter had swallowed a bottle of aspirin, but she was going to be all right.

My mother was spared from telling me. She knew I had overheard. She came into the room as I stood there, the phone still clutched against my ear, listening to the dial tone. She knew that I had heard his final words. If I ever spoke to Margaret again, he would gut me like a capon.

*　*　*

Campbell took me out that night. I was not well. I had thought it didn't matter what I did, but I was wrong. Whether the faculty that began to torment me could properly be called a conscience, I do not know; it hardly seemed orderly enough, and I felt more nausea than remorse. I believe, in fact, that it was the faculty of memory. I did what I did with Margaret only because I could forget her while I did it. It was not that I set out to cause Margaret pain. It was rather something in the architecture of desire that required a sacrifice. There was an altar, and a tradition of blood.

I thought it didn't matter what I did, because I was already damned. But damnation does not let you off the hook. Damnation precisely is the hook.

Campbell took me out of my bed, where I had curled since noon; he knew as well as I did the life-breathing fact of the night air. Mortification is this: a cloak of death you pull about you in hopes of making yourself invisible to the light and shame of your desire. Campbell did not want to see me curl up in this black cloth. Not yet. Not before he had taught me something. We would go under, this night.

There was an opening in the pavement. Campbell knew about it. Near Yonge and Queen, on a side street, there was an opening that had been paved over, but it could not be covered.

They had planned a subway line, running east and west from a transfer point at Yonge and Queen. They had even built a station, immediately below the existing station on the Yonge line. The walls were finished in the old square tiles and branded with the name of the stop; the platforms were paved and the stairways cut. Then the project was abandoned.

Now there was a phantom subway station, floating in the earth beneath the city. There was no access from the Queen station above; the stairs had been filled in. There was supposed to be no access at all. It was a rare public space: condemned to slow unoccupied ruin before it was opened to the city. A tomb at birth.

Campbell knew that a shaft led down from the street level, a circular well stapled with rungs. They had paved over the manhole, but Campbell had seen it. On certain nights—important nights, the kind that Katie talked about—the dull steel disk was fully visible in the cracked road.

It was visible on this night.

I was slow as we walked there, sick with thought. Overwhelmingly, I was recalling Margaret's innocence—not innocence in the sense of naivete, but innocence from guilt. She had done nothing. She was sweet, and devoted, and intrigued, but she had done nothing.

In the same category as my concern about damage to the soul is a question concerning seduction. If a man denies that a woman has any will in her seduction, then he is denying her will. If he insists that she is a full partner in the act, then he must somehow account for Margaret.

I knew, I simply knew, that there was a category of crime, in no legal sense rape, in which most men were implicated.

110

The dull steel lid lay folded into the road without ostentation. It might have been an ordinary manhole, except that I sensed it had not been there the day before. It had been conjured by something: by Campbell; perhaps by my crime.

Campbell had an iron bar, hammered square at the end, which fit into a square hole in the lid like a key. He pushed with his small weight against the bar and the disk lifted from the surface of the road.

"You go down first," Campbell said.

The rungs were of twisted rebar, the sinew employed to reinforce concrete. They were rough against my hands, rusted. I let myself down into the shaft, and the air became still, damp, and stale around me. The light from the street disappeared.

Campbell, climbing down above me, slipped a flashlight into my hand. "There's a system of tunnels in the Rockies, you know. Train tunnels. Huge invisible circles beneath the mountain . . ."

"Oh yeah?"

I clipped the flashlight to my belt and the beam hung down, swinging, illuminating the falling shaft below me in dizzy light. I have always suffered from vertigo, but had never shown fear in front of Campbell.

"Yeah. They were designed by a Swiss engineer. Neurotic guy, very precise. I would call him a genius, myself."

The concept of genius was very important to Campbell. He considered himself a genius, and was always trying to decide what that meant.

"You see, they had to level the steepness of the grade.

The track used to run at an unacceptable pitch; it would sometimes burn out the brakes on the trains. Runaways."

My hands were wet and becoming red, I knew, with rust; but I gripped the iron until they were white beneath the red. Campbell came down on top of me at quite a pace, and forced me to move more quickly than my terrified muscles would have chosen.

"So the solution, you see, was to carve a huge circle beneath the rock, so the train would coil around like a snake. The head of the train now comes out of the mountain just below the opening where the tail disappears."

A circle of black earth was approaching from the bottom of the shaft. I levered myself down towards it with vicelike joints, and my body relaxed into free movement only when I felt the uneven ground under my shoes.

Campbell hopped down and stood beside me. He gestured now as he spoke, conjuring.

"The circular tunnel was started at both ends. They had two crews digging, and it was the responsibility of this man—the Swiss engineer—to ensure that the semicircles would meet, precisely, in the center of the rock."

He stepped into the darkness, and continued to speak.

"Day before the semicircles were scheduled to meet, the engineer lost his nerve. He convinced himself that he had made a mistake in his calculations. The crews would never meet."

His voice echoed now; he was standing at a distance.

"They would never meet. They would pass in the dark and be lost.

"This, for a man like our engineer, was the moment of despair. The mind had failed; the meaning was lost. He put a gun to his head."

I unclipped the light and shone it about.

"In an instant of blood and smoke, he erased for ever that incomparable mind, punished it for producing a travesty of reason."

We were in the tunnel, an aborted passage complete with a few hundred feet of rail terminating in a wall of earth. At the other end it seemed to widen.

"The next day, the last few yards of rock were blasted from either side.

"The tunnels met. They met precisely, creating one tunnel, making a perfect spiral beneath the mountain. The workers from the opposing crews, who hadn't seen each other in weeks, fell into each other's arms and wept."

I shone the flashlight on Campbell; he was at the other end of the track. He spoke dramatically in an elevated voice, as if he were on stage.

"This is the kind of completeness that steals blood from the heart. It is what we refer to when we speak of genius."

I made my way to Campbell along the tracks, all the while avoiding the electrified third rail out of habit, as if it carried a powerful current.

"That the Swiss committed suicide is by no means alien to the paradigm. The expenditure of human energy, the immense concentration necessary to bring a work of genius from the small and human mind, is sufficient to deplete the will. It does not surprise us that the agent is thus open to despair, and defenseless should that terrible condition arise."

The tunnel did widen. The lip of a platform became visible, and then the ghostly tiles with the station name engraved at regular intervals. We were in a subway station. It was one of those glowing midnight encounters. Anything public has a veil of privacy at night, but this— this small part of the city had been condemned to night unbroken until the earth split and opened its secrets to the sky. It was like stumbling across the forgotten burial chamber of a pharaoh.

"But all this has changed, of course. We have a hard time conceiving of genius now, because the notion of completeness is suspect. It has been challenged. The very existence of an agent has been questioned. Now, at best we imagine two crews tunneling under the rock without guidance. There is no engineer; he died long ago. The semicircles are imprecise. They pass each other on the appointed day and they leave a huge margin of solid rock between them; they tunnel into the darkening earth, spiraling downward, alone; they create two separate spirals out of which no train could possibly emerge.

"We have forgotten what completeness is. The word 'genius' sounds false in our ears."

I stood in front of Campbell, but I did not want to appear to be listening too seriously. The word "genius," for Campbell, was inextricable from some contemplated criminal act. When he spoke in this way, obsessively, with increasingly formal precision, I knew that he was planning something. He was making me nervous. So I

114

faced the other way, pretending great interest in what I could illuminate with the powerful beam.

"Our concern, now, is for the train. Where does it go? We have seen it disappear into the earth, and we know that it cannot emerge."

He paused, for a long time. When he spoke it was in a low voice, sad, yet somehow infinitely threatening.

"We know that the crews are lost. That the tunnels will never meet. And we wonder what will happen to that burrowing, unhappy train."

The silence that followed was different. It was somehow more complete. I turned around.

Campbell was gone. A moment before he had been standing behind me—I could hear him breathing—and now he was gone. I tried his name, whispering: "Campbell?"

He did not respond. Suddenly overcome with an irrational fear—I was standing in the middle of a subway track—I pulled myself up over the lip of the platform and lay for a moment on the polished floor. "Campbell?"

The silence was uncanny. I expected something, perhaps the slow dripping of stalactites.

At certain moments, either moments of perfectly lucid thought or utter confusion, I find myself questioning the most basic things. I find myself tapping on the floor, to see whether it is indeed solid, strong enough to hold me up. Was this boy really my friend? What, for instance, if he were not? What then? I was always afraid to ask this kind of question, in case it was a product of confusion. Then the disloyalty would be mine.

115

What did I know about Campbell, after all? That he was there, one day, unbidden. Why should he not leave in the same way? This talk of trains, and genius: what was he concocting?

No matter which part of the cavernous space I illuminated, there would always be a much greater cave of blackness over my shoulder. I began to swing the light, wildly, in hopes of catching whatever might try to approach in darkness, and then I realized the irrationality of my behavior. Campbell would be able to see this if he were hiding somewhere within sight. Was this what he wanted to see?

A cold murmur of steel on steel shook the platform at my feet. It must be the train on the line above, I thought. I kept the light now fixed in one direction, before me, as I walked to the opposite end of the platform. "Campbell?"

There was a stair at the far end. Would it lead somewhere? Was Campbell perhaps there? The need to make the situation ring true allowed me to embrace the wildest assumptions: that Campbell had merely wandered off, that he couldn't hear me because he was too far away.

The rattle of heavy steel wheels was more audible now.

I began to step up the stairway. It went at least around one bend at the landing, beyond which I could not see. "Campbell?"

I stood on the landing and aimed the flashlight up the second flight of stairs. A ring of yellow light on a stringy patch of earth. They had plugged the passage with soil, as if it were a grave. I turned quickly.

The ringing was still distant, but I could hear it. A subway train. With a certain kind of terror comes clarity, however, and I remembered: there were no subway trains at this hour. The last train was at perhaps two in the morning, and it was much later than that.

Perhaps I should leave. This thought had not yet occurred to me because I had not until now allowed myself truly to imagine the possibility that something was going on, had been intended from the start.

I am uncommonly sane, I suppose. I do not scream out, or rarely, because there is always a reason for everything, and screaming rarely cures the situation. I was not screaming now, although I was feeling the same vertigo on flat ground that I had felt at the top of the ladder. I began to walk, slowly, towards the other end of the platform.

Stairs emerged from the wall at the side of the platform, but I gave them a wide berth. Campbell had told me, after all, that the stairs were blocked. It was not so unusual to discover that they indeed were. Why did I now look back over everything Campbell had ever said to me, picking through it for lies?

I sat on the edge of the platform, preparing to lower myself. The sound had been growing for some time, and I was experiencing a sudden unreasonable fear. It was like my unnecessary avoidance of the third rail: suddenly I thought better of my plan to walk the brief passage of track to the source of the ladder.

117

I pulled my feet back up onto the platform—too quickly, I suppose, if somebody were watching.

The sound had an insistent quality to it now: it was not the kind of sound one heard through a thick wall of solid earth; it was a strong acoustical sound, the kind that echoed in a tunnel, say, in which one was standing. Feeling foolish, I stepped back from the end of the platform.

There was a wind in my hair. Impossible. The sound had risen now to an unbroken roar. I put my hands over my ears, as if that might ward off the coming scream, but despite myself, I found myself screaming.

It did not stop at the platform, but thundered by without mercy. Old and red, with the gray-green interiors and circular frosted lights that I remembered from my childhood.

I stood there, long after it had passed and the sound had died to an echo. I stood there, thinking. I was not worried for Campbell: he would not have been on the tracks when it came through. Whatever he did, I now saw, was too thoughtful, too carefully premeditated for that kind of mistake. I, on the other hand, had intended to walk towards the ladder. Staring out over the space, I wondered again about the third rail. Certain potencies are invisible. You simply feel them, too late, when you stumble into their path.

I did not see Campbell again, not for years.

In Campbell's absence, the Friends deferred to the authority of the silent Lewis. His reticence became a theme: nobody mentioned Campbell's name. It was as if Campbell had never been one of us; as if the crime had not been his invention. I was certainly not going to say anything about that night. The manhole had been open when I found my way back up, sick by then with terror as well as remorse, and I was safe—why should the Friends know anything about my particular humiliation? It was odd, however, that in Campbell's absence my authority seemed to dwindle.

Lewis occasionally whispered something in Cran's ear; this was the only sign that he was in control. The garrulous Cran did almost all of the speaking, all of the organizing. Ainsley simply sat back and took it all in, sometimes smiling that monstrous smile when a certain aspect of the proposed crime struck him as unusually ingenious.

I had been given the privileged position on the periphery with Campbell. Now that Campbell was gone, however, this position did not seem such a privilege: I was clearly excluded. Though I had some sense of what was to happen, I had been reduced to a complicitous observer. When some of the more surprising details were revealed, after the fact, I understood why I had been placed where I was.

The bank was a neoclassical structure facing Yonge Street. It looked like the Pantheon made narrow, as if it had been filmed to be projected on a wide screen but was bent through the wrong lens. All of the gods. A much narrower structure now suited the pantheon, of course; they could squeeze in between the tellers without much discomfort.

I was positioned in a fast food outlet across the street,

where I melted in with other waiting criminals: grunting hunched adolescents who would sell you their girlfriends. I looked out over an elevated red counter, through a pane of glass smeared with grease.

The facade of the bank was calm and ludicrous in the market atmosphere of the night. Girls no more than fourteen clutched long purses without handles under their armpits, a symbol that they were yours for a small price. Or a large price, depending on how you looked at it. Boys wandered up and down, their pockets stuffed with dust and spices; for a price they would split your mind and sew it back together with dissolving thread.

The bank seemed oblivious. Ainsley was already inside; he had been since the bank closed that afternoon. I had only a vague idea, as I say, of the details, but I knew this: Ainsley had seduced the assistant manager. She was an introverted woman, with a good heart but a face to freeze blood, and it was difficult for her to reject Ainsley's advances, unsavory though he was: there was a good chance nothing better would ever come along. Ainsley had often visited her after-hours in the vault, so he knew the terrain. And he had duplicates of all of her keys.

Cran's black limousine drifted silently into view. He had picked up a long winged wreck from a graveyard of metal, painted it black and replaced the engine; it was huge, and rode on its soft suspension like a tank. He parked across the street from the bank, a few doors down from my window.

I had not been permitted to monitor the earlier stage of the operation: Cran, on Campbell's instructions, had made his way into a low apartment building, some-where in the suburbs, where he had found a key, in an envelope, in a drawer. The key had been placed there some thirty years before and had not been touched since. It was one of two keys required to open a certain safety deposit box. The other was in Ainsley's hand.

Cran, brimming over with the energy of remaining silent, made his way through moving cars to the bank, leaving Lewis almost invisible in the back seat of the black tank.

Dressed as a caretaker and pulling an industrial vacuum cleaner behind him, Ainsley opened the front door of the bank to permit Cran's entrance. That smile.

I turned away and examined my colleagues at the red counter. Their skin was uniformly scarred, ravaged by adolescence and vile food; they spoke to each other in strong conspiratorial whispers, only raising their voices when something important was meant to be overheard by a member of the opposite sex. I watched them, lis-tened to their painful rehearsed remarks, and tried to forget that what I was now involved in, the crime in which I was now implicated, would be far more serious than anything I had ever contemplated before.

Yes, Campbell had planned it, and it was doubtful that anything would go truly wrong: Ainsley and his un-fortunate accomplice would have disengaged every alarm, would have turned every camera away from the neces-sary doors; but I was uneasy. I had been left out of this, and I did not know the details. I simply did not know.

"Pssst!"

It was Cran, standing at my shoulder, shivering with the rigor of silence; I followed him out to the floating car. In the back were Lewis and Ainsley, and there was gold in their hands. It was over.

As we moved down and away from Yonge Street, Cran broke into a stream of exultant chatter: "Watches, we got watches, thousands of little watches, we can wear a different watch every day for the rest of our lives and never run out of time . . ."

Somebody had filled a deep safety deposit box with a collection of priceless timepieces, tiny jeweled mechanisms in heavy gold cases. Ainsley swung one from a thick chain and smiled slowly.

As I sat in the rabbi's office with my parents during the few quiet minutes before the ceremony, I thought about Campbell and the Friends. After the crime—which had gone beautifully, I thought, without repercussions—the Friends had also disappeared. I had not seen Ainsley, Lewis, or Cran for over a month. The stolen watches had disappeared with them, which I did not mind so much: I was never in it for the take. But I was now more alone than I had been for years.

It was difficult to concentrate on the ceremony ahead of me. The rabbi was saying something about a mitzvah: how he encouraged young boys to balance out the worldly excess of a modern bar mitzvah by devoting themselves quietly to a charitable work. He was suggesting, more to my parents than to me, that the Jewish hospital required volunteers, and that something of this nature might be appropriate. Though I was not listening, my mother would remind me of the rabbi's suggestion later, and it would seem peculiarly appropriate: by then, it would seem an act of penance.

I looked about me, nervously. Abba was supposed to be here; he had been invited to join this quiet chat in the rabbi's office, and I was surprised that he was absent. My mother, too, seemed nervous about this. She kept looking at her watch.

The rabbi's office was in a private section of the synagogue, where the bureaucracy was housed. The stained teak shelves held a vast collection of books: volumes of the Talmud, modern interpretive works, the very latest research in self-help and popular psychology.

I went over my portion in my mind. It was all there. The prayers, the melodies. I was ready.

The rabbi was still talking to my parents. My mother listened intently, but my father stared at the ceiling. My father was trying to be respectful, but he did not seem to have reserves of actual respect to draw upon. As a result, he had lapsed from the start into an informal cordiality with the rabbi, as if they were friends, or business acquaintances. Every once in a while, my father would drop his front completely: for instance, when the rabbi suggested that the whole family should be taking a more active role in the religious community. My father frowned at this, although I am sure he did not mean to—he had narrowed his eyes in a way that suggested barely restrained violence. The rabbi trod more carefully after seeing that look.

As far as I could tell, the rabbi was a good man: what Misha would call a good Jew. Thin and groomed in his blue suit, he looked like a benevolent accountant, and from what he said, you could tell his heart flowed over. He cared a lot, for instance, about everything. He was the kind of man you could imagine caring a lot about trees, and very small animals, and bad poetry. It was difficult to dislike the rabbi, although I found myself, like my father, not wanting to listen to him—it was difficult as well to conjure up real respect.

In five minutes we were to enter the Great Chapel. My mother expressed concern for Abba. He was driving to the synagogue, alone, though Mother had offered to pick him up. Had something happened on the road?

Abba did not drive the way my mother drove. He was not so much aware, behind the wheel, as charmed. He had never taken a driving lesson in his life, and had driven without mishap for over sixty years. As long as he felt the car would come to no harm, it would not. Nevertheless, whenever he was late, we worried.

An anxious knock on the rabbi's door was followed by Abba's flushed appearance in the room. He seemed uncharacteristically nervous, and his face was etched with red veins, as if his blood were pushing against the surface. "I'm sorry," he said. "I'm sorry I'm late."

And then he took my hand. "I'm sorry, Isaac."

Why was he sorry? He hadn't missed anything. My mother touched his shoulder. Abba looked out the window and began to speak in a voice of quiet distress.

"I had a gift for you, Isaac. I was going to bring it with me this morning." He paused. "Something terrible has happened."

124

My mother was on her feet, trying to peer into Abba's eyes. He looked away.

"I'm sorry," he said. "This is not the right time to talk about it." He forced a smile. "You're going to be bar mitzvahed, Isaac. This is a special occasion."

My mother pressed his arm. "What?"

Abba was silent for a moment. I noticed that the rabbi had sunk into a quiet confusion of his own: something real had intruded upon the false calm of his office, and he was unnerved.

Abba at last turned to me. "I have a collection of watches, Isaac. Old watches—good ones—they were my inheritance. My great-grandfather was a collector. He passed his collection on to his son, who passed it on to my father, who passed it on to me."

The Torah portion was cycling through my mind now, turning over like the ticks of an engine, a rhythmic litany, anything to stay calm.

"One of those watches, on a thick gold chain, is priceless: it is the most valuable thing I own. It was going to be your gift, Isaac."

The rabbi stood. "We have to move into the chapel now," he said.

Abba remained still; nobody else in the family stood. "I went to my safety deposit box this morning," Abba said, "where I keep it. The collection." He paused, and then looked at me sorrowfully, with eyes that begged understanding. "I'm sorry, Isaac. There has been a theft."

Josh was staring at me, with a hard look I had never seen.

*　*　*

As I stood on the platform behind the altar, I was unaware of the many eyes focused upon me. I had gone back into my mind; I was sifting through the blackened facts of my life for evidence.

Campbell. What had I done, that he would do this to me? There had been the moments of humiliation—certainly I had tested him—but all in the spirit of friendship, I thought. As I recited my Torah portion from memory, I fought to remember Campbell precisely, so that I might reinterpret his character. I had tried to do this on the night he had disappeared. And try as I might, the best I could produce was the possibility that he had more pride than he showed, that he had become my disciple in hopes of winning absolute respect, that he had failed, and taken revenge.

The rabbi was looking at me strangely. I was coming to the end of my portion; my recitation had been flawless. And what about the other Friends? Was I wrong to assume that they were there for me? Were they Campbell's people? The rabbi touched my hand, tentatively, as I finished my portion. I looked out over the audience. Misha was there—he seemed horrified. Abba was looking at the floor, but then he had suffered a terrible shock.

And then, in a moment sick with immediate knowledge, I understood: I had recited the entire portion in reverse. Of course the rest of the congregation were smiling with pride. Abba, Misha, and the rabbi were the only ones there who knew Hebrew.

When it came time to sing the next prayer, my voice cracked and disappeared.

Josh took Abba's arm at the end of the ceremony, to help him to his car; neither of them would meet my eyes. I wish I had spoken to them, explained—though I was to find out soon that Josh already knew. He had written everything down in clean prose before it had ever happened. I simply wish I had said it, myself; that might have lifted the pall. Within minutes, it was too late.

We were told at the reception. The guests were still filing in, with gifts, shaking my hand, when the rabbi rushed up to my mother, in tears.

Abba and Josh had become lost. Abba had driven the wrong way, as if he were trying to leave the city rather than come to the reception; Josh was in the seat beside him. The driver behind was convinced it was a terrible mistake, but a conscious decision nevertheless—Abba had put on the left-turn indicator, and turned. But there was no road to the left. Only a thin rail that bent and snapped like a ribbon. Especially surprising to the police and the insurance company was that the car had burst into flame in the arc of its descent, and had burned for some minutes on the green shoulder before it could be approached.

There was no reason for this.

I became calm. Even at the funeral, I felt as if I had been lifted outside of society. I felt as if I were walking the floor of a white lunar sea and breathing an air that no one else could breathe.

When Aaron found out, he left the reception in silence. Many people later told the rabbi that they had seen a young boy that afternoon, in tears, his back against the wall of the synagogue, straining with all his might. And certainly a wall of the synagogue had been ruined, inexplicably, pulled straight out of its foundations and lifted until it broke away and crumbled.

3

HOSPITAL

Woe unto them that join house to house, that lay field to field, till there be no place, that they may be placed alone in the midst of the earth.
In mine ears said the Lord of hosts, Of a truth many houses shall be desolate, even great and fair, without inhabitant.

Isaiah 5:8–9

THE STORY WAS BROKEN NOW. Josh had told our story; he had made sense of us, pieced us into the narrative and given us meaning, and now his voice was gone. Without Josh, you see, we were afraid that the language of the family—that the family itself, really—would be fractured.

He left notes, which my mother began to read the day after his death: partial notes, towards a complete story. Within them could be discerned numerous possibilities, few of them happy: ways in which our lives might go, if we could fill in the missing chapters. Not surprisingly, the notes did not suggest any one direction that we might all go together. They did, however, stress one partner in my life, a woman I had never met. A woman named Katie.

I remember the first time I had the courage to enter Josh's room after the accident. I no longer turned to the library—any library—and I missed written confirmation of the world about me. Relations around the dinner table were becoming incomprehensible, and I would find myself staring at the scars in the surface of the wood, hoping to read something there.

My mother began to do unsettling things. One month, she served lamb every evening for thirty-one nights in a row. Towards the end of this period, my father began to yell at her. You could see that he didn't want to, not only because it was a sign that he was no longer as contained as he once was but because he was in fact a compassionate man. He had come to the decision, though, that he was not happy with us. The family was beginning to seem to him a prison of absurdity, a lawless place, which was mocking the rational effort of his life.

"I have welded my life to yours," he was really saying as he yelled. "Why are you serving lamb again?" If you listened closely to the content of his rant, this is the sense that emerged: "You are connected to me, and going bad, like a dying limb."

I would never have said anything. Neither would Aaron. Lamb was Josh's favorite food, and Aaron had preserved a core of reverence for Josh's memory.

My father, however, could not take it any more. He had never liked lamb at the best of times.

His first explosion was preceded by a moment of unusual calm. My mother had just served the lamb. A roast of lamb; it was well into the third week of this. She placed the roast in front of my father to carve. It lay, in a mint sauce, on the oblong carving board Mother had inherited from Abba. The thick wooden platter had grooves cut in it so that the juices would flow in an orderly way and collect in a round pool at one end. My father usually made a great show of sharpening the carving knife against its matching sharpener, a long cylinder of roughened stainless steel on an elegant handle. But today he left the knife and its sharpener in their wooden case.

He picked up the roast in his bare hands. He stood, slowly, contemplating the roast lamb, which was staining his hands with juice. His fingers curled tensely about the meat, but he said nothing. We waited.

He looked down at my mother, who stared back with perfect equanimity. And he began to shout.

"I hate lamb! I hate it ! I can't stand it! I like pork. Liver. Beef. I cannot stand lamb!"

Then he placed the lamb back on the heavy platter and began to carve.

The rest of the meal progressed without event, but I felt a need, afterwards, to examine the flaws that were appearing in the behavior of my parents.

I repaired to Josh's room. Mother spent a great deal of time in there; she told us that she was reading Josh's notes, and that we might wish to, but that we must always leave them where we found them, whether on the floor, taped to walls, or filed away. She sensed an order in their arrangement, as if the room had the shape of a book.

I went in, seeking an answer to the question raised: would my family survive?

Josh's room was like a library after a small explosion. There was paper everywhere: nailed to the walls, stuffed under the bed, clinging to the ceiling with bits of yellowing tape. I would not wish to catalog that work, but I did come away with the same sense that my mother had—that the room was possessed of order, that there was a narrative—though I felt that entering that room was less like opening a book than stepping onto a theatrical stage, where meaning was evident in every dimension.

There were rhymes, which seemed to make sense of the notes the way that a table of contents details the structure of a book. Everything else was written in the first person, though in voices that changed: I recognized not only my own peculiar way of putting words together but also inner modes of speech that, though alien, I knew must belong to the other members of my family. Only one voice was missing, as far as I could discern, and that was Josh's own.

This marked the first period in my life in which I could not read. Try as I might to follow any one narrative stream, I found my attention wavering; I would forget the beginning of the page by the time I had come to the end; I would be convinced I could no longer understand the simplest sentences; I would give up in despair. Though I spent hours in Josh's room, I did not come away with much: fragments, names, omens.

For three years until I met Katie, this was the case.

It was only with great difficulty that I managed to pick up books again, when I was sixteen, at the university. At first I merely sat in on classes, but after some time with Katie I had the courage to try reading. I was not good at it. In some important sense, I had to learn all over, but when I saw what they did to Katie—how she would never be able to read again—I was determined that I would force myself.

Aaron had been accepted into engineering and would begin the next year. Not merely engineering, but Engineering Science, an elite subfaculty with a less regimented but far more demanding curriculum. Many of Aaron's courses would consist of single projects: he would be told to build an airplane, or to design a small nuclear generator, and it would be his task to learn the theory and practice on his own with minimal guidance. If the airplane flew, if the generator fed power to the city, he would pass.

Though my father was in mourning, he was secretly thrilled. Aaron the renegade would have a profession, and engineering in particular appealed to my father's sensibilities. Medicine had pretensions to saintliness— this irritated my father; lawyers did not get their hands dirty, and my father was a builder; engineers, on the other hand, were at the center of his world. Any substantial improvement in the technique of engineering would inevitably save my father money; also, he genuinely admired the mental rigor of the many engineers with whom he associated. They could do things that he could never do. Aaron was going to be not merely an engineer, my father would later brag, but a prince among engineers.

My brother accepted the congratulations with wry pleasure, though he too was in mourning. His school had taught him that he could do whatever he wished in society—it was his playground—so he was not in the least surprised that he had been accepted into an elite faculty at the university. He was, however, quietly pleased that he had made such a popular choice.

Nor was he overly anxious about the competition he would face. He knew that the average student in his class would swim through calculus like water, would be highly motivated and ruthless; but he also knew that most of them would be stunted in crucial areas of life. Aaron had been trained to be a leader of men. He could lift heavy objects, and he was incidentally a wizard with machines. It would be no contest.

Aaron had a girlfriend now, a serious young woman from Fulsome Hall, the most prestigious private school for girls. Anne would be studying biology and chemistry, and hoped very much to pursue a career in medicine. If they slept together—and I imagine they did—it was not momentous: their lives were focused upon more important things.

Aaron disdained me even more than before, if that was possible. His position in the private club of his future had now been secured; he was safely part of the group he wanted to know, and I was little more than an embarrassment from his past.

I must confess that I cared less about Aaron myself. I had my own ideas, inherited from Mr. Arrensen, and later filtered through the superior teachings of a subtle tyrant I would meet at the university, Professor Abraham Gold. I saw engineers as narrow, arrogant, and doomed: specialized men, blasphemers, even in a world without God, and destined at some point to confront the true horror of their creations, like Mary Shelley's good doctor.

A clean corridor of hospitals lined University Avenue. Following the rabbi's advice, I volunteered myself to the newest and cleanest of these, a Jewish hospital thick with the wires of medicine. The buildings were bound together by an arterial network of underground passages; the circuits in the walls flowed without interruption into the veins of the patients, a natural systemic whole. Life was supported here.

I was given a job in the first-floor cafeteria. It was a public cafeteria, a meeting place between the privileged sick, their doctors, and the hale world of street-level Toronto. I met all kinds.

The food suffered beneath shrink wrap for hours, and lost its nature. Food poisoning was always a problem, as in most hospitals; the kitchen was as large and impersonal as an insurance company. The doctors and nurses, who subsisted on this food and rarely slept, were as pale as the patients.

The mobile sick were sometimes allowed to meet visitors in the ground-floor lobby. After months of confinement on the ward, the patients would welcome this ordinary cafeteria as an exquisite luxury; they would issue their friends into the lineup with excited smiles, and I would often overhear them discussing the food with the sensitivity of gourmet diners: *You simply must taste the osso bucco.*

I was invisible among them. Where cleanliness is a cardinal virtue—Zurich, Toronto, hospitals—waste becomes something shameful, and the collectors of waste a class of untouchables. I was there to remove the unsightly trays, the residue of once-packaged meals.

Invisibility suited me fine. Where there were veins in the eyes, mine flowed with milk. There was no blood in my vision any more. All I saw were transparencies, and I was happy to be seen as one myself.

Many things were missing from the hospital, but what I missed more than anything else was music. I did not understand how important music was until I was punished with silence; nobody in the family, in fact, had properly understood the importance of Josh. Though he had kept his distance—we had all kept our distance—he had made sense of us. He was the melody. He wove sense into whatever we would have been without him—chaos, cacophony, silence—and now that he was gone, any one of these alternatives seemed possible.

I was content to be a fixture in the hospital, wired into the pulse of the circuit, because those walls defined a new kind of life: a life without Josh. I was part of the hospital now, and it would sustain me even though I never heard music again.

My volunteer work in the hospital introduced me to a way of being that would suit me well for the next few years as I found my way through a tangle of self-recrimination: I was least unhappy where I was unknown, marginal, anonymous, invisible.

A line of nameless women shuffled through the cafeteria, muttering, unconscious of themselves, barely dressed, as if it were their private kitchen. They had been prodded and poked by cold hands until they had become creatures without sex, the animal shells of human beings, relieved of pride and dignity and the rigors of public shame. All of them had stories; I knew that. Like mine, however, their personal storyteller had died, or perhaps gone away, leaving their days listless and similar and white.

History departs in the emergency room. In its place they issue a card and a bracelet. These women had become the perfect citizens of the modern city: clinging to life, and nothing else. Their prayers became simple. They would pray to the humming wires about them for painless, comfortable, extended life. And the wires, unlike the god who had forsaken them outside, would listen.

She, however, was immediately different. I was sixteen when I saw her first, and I had been working in the hospital for three years. It was an ordinary day, a white hospital day; the world around me was making the motions of chewing, was slow, slack-jawed, and white. She spread across the gauze of my vision like a spill of brilliant dye.

It was the only constant with her: the uncanny effect she had upon the world around her. She colored everything in her path with her childlike affect. If she was happy, the room was ecstatic; if she was sad, the entire community despaired. People who did not know her would find themselves pulled into the emotions of her life, simply because she had walked by.

She opened into my lunar sea like a wave of blood.

This woman never ordered food. She never stood in line. She merely sat there, every second day or so, and experienced the public life on the first floor. Once, I had reason to pick up a tray at her left elbow, and I brushed against the fine surface of her arm. It was like being crippled.

I wanted her with a kind of desire I had not felt since that first day of Margaret; I felt as if I had come full circle; her hair was clean and light.

Of all the people sitting in that cafeteria, she was the only one who had not become part of the bleaching agenda of health. She was profoundly sick in her soul; she was in some kind of unreachable pain. She was not going to be cured.

For months, I collected trays about her, and said nothing.

I began to spend entire days at the university. Perhaps it was because I knew that the only road out of my sunken life was a spark of desire, and the university was, sexually, by far the most strong and perverse community I had ever encountered. Not simply the social atmosphere, which was of course full of manipulation and lust, but learning itself was a path of sexual violence, and there were quiet places in the university where students actually learned.

I had never graduated from high school, but nobody complained when I began to audit classes. I looked old for sixteen, sickly and numb; I did not seem out of place.

One professor in particular was noted for the degree of loyalty he inspired in his students: they followed him, after a year in his class, with the docile devotion of lovers—or rather, as if they had been raped and then blackmailed into submission. He gathered supporters about him, and did to their minds what I did to Margaret in the stairwell. Professor Gold had become powerful in the ranks of the university.

I was fascinated by the tiny social history of the place: the small wars, the hatred. Gold had risen to his place in this little pantheon, I knew, by exploiting the intellectual demise of a powerful rival.

Students still talked about the spectacular fall of Professor Beacham. He had conjured fear and wonder in his glory days, precisely because he denied his students the consummation of their allegiance: he was distant. Beacham adhered to a Viennese doctrine, now dominant in England and America, that denied, essentially, that anything human was important. He taught that faith was a psychological trap, love an extension of the hormones, the good life impossible to know, unworthy of theory and best relegated to the arbiters of popular prejudice. The most vicious word in his vocabulary, and there were many, was "metaphysics."

More than one graduate student had seen six years of doctoral work dismissed at the end of an oral defense as "metaphysics." By "metaphysics," Professor Beacham meant whatever was soft, rather than hard; whatever strayed beyond the interpretation of concrete sensible data; whatever could not be seen, but merely felt. Professor Beacham saw himself as a lone soldier laying waste the realm of the invisible.

His position was irrefutable. Many students felt that he must be wrong, but they always found themselves with the greater burden of proof. His world was hard and visible, theirs no more palpable than the wind. They would call witnesses without voices. Worse of all, they found themselves incurring not merely Professor Beacham's indifference—which was generously made available to all—but his disdain.

Professor Beacham had departed by the time I arrived at the university. From what I could determine, however, students had coveted his love as much as they now did Professor Gold's. The difference was this: Beacham made his love valuable, by offering it to none; Gold made his love a perpetual focus, by making it painful and contradictory. Both were tyrants.

The signs that Professor Beacham was on the decline were at first subtle. He would be giving a class on Russell, or Quine, and he would suddenly lapse into a language that had never been heard before. Since it was unthinkable to correct the professor, the entire class would suffer through an incomprehensible lecture.

Once a young Beachamite invited a girlfriend to audit a class. She, a major in Classics, was uniquely capable of recognizing the arcane language that Beacham slipped into, in a moment of uncustomary rhetorical fervor: it was ancient Greek.

For an entire afternoon, one day, she sat there. I was in a fever all the while. I carried my trays with the suspicion that my skin was on fire, that there was a fire on my skin that the world could see. At the end of the afternoon, she smiled at me.

She had never smiled specifically at me before. She had smiled in an all-inclusive way, which incidentally took me into its sphere, but she had never smiled exclusively at me. Not knowing what I was doing, burning in the confusion of her color, I sat down beside her.

I sat for a long time, and she remained where she was. I think she looked at me, but I was staring at the table in front of me, so hard that I feared it might melt, and I could see nothing else.

At last I looked up, and between teeth welded in fear, I said, "My name's Izzy."

She said nothing, but put a hand to her throat, and I understood: she could not speak.

Professor Beacham should not have known ancient Greek. He had been campaigning for years to have funds transferred from the Classics department into the more needy faculties. Applied Mathematics, for instance, was growing fast, and hungry. He had little use for Latin, and less for Greek; thus it was a surprise that he spoke Greek fluently. And not simple Greek. He spoke in a sparse, epigrammatic style that the Classics student had no trouble identifying with a specific period in the lengthy history of that language: his Greek would have made him eloquent in the fifth century before Christ. As it was, his fluency was perplexing, and for the younger students, who depended upon his lectures so that they might pass their exams, aggravating.

The graduate students were by no means unanimous in their approach to Beacham's new tendency. They were roughly split into two camps. The first group was convinced that he was losing it, that he had been staring for years into matters too deep (or too shallow) to be contemplated without despair, and that he had become incoherent by virtue of that very condition. The second group was more cagey. In their eyes, the professor had recently experienced an epiphany, as a result of which his views had changed radically, and his new and inscrutable behavior was a calculated pedagogical technique: a dramatic means of issuing in a new era of thought, which the students would do well to comprehend if they were at all concerned for the future of their careers.

In a sense, both camps were right. Professor Beacham was not only uttering the language of his personal despair; he was also heralding the birth of a new regime. He was announcing the impending tyranny of Professor Gold.

I learned from a sentence scrawled on a paper place mat that her name was Katie. Katie. The name had come up in Joshua's notes, which were sometimes written in my voice. I had never made a proper study of the notes, not only because my reading skills were failing but because what little I read there filled me with self-loathing. The pieces in my voice were a memoir of my life, past and future, and they read like a verdict.

Thus I did not know what to expect from this Katie, except that she figured prominently in my future reminiscence.

Our first few weeks of friendship passed in silence, which neither of us seemed to mind. Why could she not speak? I asked her, and she shrugged her shoulders. But she smiled at me, often now, and I convinced myself that she came to the cafeteria to be with me, that she liked my company.

If I look back over this early time, when neither words nor actions clouded my rapport with Katie, I realize that it was the beginning of my emergence from the fugue. In the quiet absence of Josh, my life had sunk beneath the level of sleep. Katie was changing that. She was apparent, concrete, color: she was the floor I had searched for in Campbell and the Friends, and she was happy to sit beside me, saying nothing. I did not immediately want any specific thing from Katie, not even conversation; I simply wanted her to be there. I was weak, then, and my needs were minimal.

If man is a social animal, perhaps this is why: the mere breathing presence of another human being is necessary to prevent the psyche from fragmenting. Without this presence we split in two, we create company within us to keep from being alone, and the tearing apart is both painful and hard to repair. Either that or we begin to die, and that was what was happening to me, alone after the bar mitzvah: I was slipping over into the world I would occupy when my body was gone.

Students from both camps could be found huddled together in gloom the day that Beacham's teaching career came to an official close.

The great man had been discovered by a maid. He was sitting in the center of his office floor, naked and caked with dung. He was tossing his books into a burning pile in front of him, a growing bonfire that was beginning to singe the ceiling. Professor Beacham fixed the startled maid with a fierce and probing eye, and pronounced (in Greek that was later deciphered): "Even here there are gods."

A quotation from Heidegger was daubed on the ceiling at an impossible height. Painted in human excrement, it had been baked by the fire until the words fused with the plaster and proved difficult to remove. "Nothing religious is ever destroyed by logic; it is destroyed only by God's withdrawal."

I don't know what I expected Katie to say when her voice returned. I did not, however, expect her to say what she did.

"Have you ever made love to another man?"

She had made love to another woman. A girl, really. When they were both fourteen. They practiced kissing, to prepare for boys; and then they found that it was a compelling activity in itself, and soon they were kissing each other everywhere, without misgiving.

As she told me this, I nodded, as if it were perfectly reasonable that she was suddenly talking, after weeks of silence, and that she was talking about this.

The other girl had finally gone off with a real boy, and Katie had returned to her room, apparently no less innocent than she had been. She still felt very much a virgin and was quite sure she was a good girl.

The reason she was telling me this now, it came out, was that she was being made to feel peculiar about that early encounter, as if it was perhaps somehow responsible for her deep misery now. "Do you think it is?" she asked me.

I did not think so. It seemed to make her feel better.

In retrospect, there were other indicators that Beacham was on the way out.

There was the business of the dog. He had been found speaking to his dog—a Scottish terrier—on more than one occasion, asking its opinion on subtle and important matters. Although he denied that these were serious chats, his detractors would insist that an important core of his doctrine could be explained only in terms of the canine influence.

There was the death of Marie, a quiet woman from Trois-Rivières whose lengthy thesis had been dismissed by Beacham as "metaphysics." She had been found hanging from an iron balustrade in the front hall of the graduate residence, and even Professor Beacham was said to have discolored slightly at the news.

Those same detractors noted in retrospect a certain detail in his relations with Marie. He had punished her, regularly, with something more than mere indifference or disdain; he had shamed her publicly at least once a week. Though nobody was suggesting an actual indiscretion, there were hints that such behavior indicated an unusual fondness, an attraction towards the shy student that was not purely professional. These hints, coupled with the possible discoloration of his features at the news of her suicide, were not altogether damning, but they were seen as a body of circumstantial evidence from which the unkind might draw conclusions.

At any rate, Professor Beacham was removed from his position by means of a glorious ceremony to which he was not expressly invited and did not find out about until the next day. He was promoted to a position that required him neither to publish nor to teach, and his office was moved out to the suburbs.

The next day, an ad hoc search committee emerged from a surprisingly brief meeting with glazed eyes and startling news: they had chosen a successor. A Professor Abraham Gold.

Katie told me about her visitor. I can only begin to describe the anguish I felt as I listened. Even to know that she had opened her robe for the fingers of an anonymous man was enough to make me almost sick with the vastness of possibility and despair.

Her white gown, with the faded hospital mark stamped above her left breast, served little more purpose than the acres of clinging drapery about the figures in the Elgin Marbles: every line and fold in her shape was perfectly evident. I felt like Michelangelo, who could see through clothes. Her figure was still round and soft: her breasts and thighs touched at points where those of the emaciated women in the hospital did not. And her face too was round and kind with suffering. Many times I felt as if I ought merely to reach out and touch her, as if it would be the most natural act in the world, as if she were asking me to do precisely this with her story of windows and moonlight. But then I would be overcome with the reality of the situation: I was just a boy. Katie was a woman of the most profound and subtle experience, and I was just a boy with leaden hands and grotesque passions.

"I can't tell you, Izzy, what that month was like. He made me into a bottle, you know. That's what he did. He filled me full of liquid and put a seal on my lips. I was just dying to . . . let out, you know. To let something out. I used to be such a perfect girl, so much in control, but I would have given anything just to be able to say his name. Or to have him touch me. He never touched all of me, you know . . . I just wanted him to touch me."

Katie put a cigarette to her lips. She had a cheap plastic lighter that was powder blue, and she was always losing it.

"Do you have a light, Izzy? Do you? Thanks, love." She put the little flame to her cigarette, then absentmindedly placed my lighter in her gown pocket.

"Maybe you don't know what it's like. For years it's so easy to keep from letting the boys get too close. You just develop this sense of humor and laugh and pull away whenever one tries to put his hand on your leg. And then suddenly you want that hand, you want it inside you . . ."

I was feeling dizzy.

"You just want to give up everything that you've guarded for so long, and you think it must be tremendously valuable because everybody's wanted it for so long, and then you discover that there's one man who . . ."

She drew upon her cigarette, to hide the pain in her face.

"Who doesn't seem to want it very badly at all. Who doesn't think you're worth all that much."

"Katie, no. I'm sure you're just . . ."

I put a hand on her leg. She neither giggled nor pulled away.

"I'm just what? Imagining things? They think I'm imagining things."

We all knew who *they* were.

"That's not what I meant."

"I know, Izzy." She put a hand on mine. "I don't know why he did . . . what he did to me."

Professor Gold was hugely obese, with folds of skin everywhere: great lidded eyes, webbed hands, breasts like a woman. He wore black tailored suits and dark ties, though he did not appear the least funereal; he looked like Bacchus, thinly disguised as an aging fascist.

His eyes glittered in a way that at first seemed friendly, and then mocking; they were surprisingly youthful in the sagging wealth of his face. His hair was full, and straight, and combed back over his shoulders with some liquid that hardened and shone.

When he met a male student for the first time, he would always shake his hand. He would hold the student's hand in his own for an unusually long time, staring the boy down. How the student responded to this initial trial, caught in the flesh of Gold's rubbery hand, determined the course of their relationship.

Women were greeted with an abstract smile. Women, for Professor Gold, were never more intrusive than a good waitress.

I found myself caught in that handshake, and I remember being able to keep my eyes focused on his, though I was flushed with alternating impulses of loathing and wonder. When he at last let my hand go, my back was wet.

Whether he had me properly figured out from that moment, I do not know. I was malleable, surely; but could he have known then that there was a flaw in my soul and my family, an impediment to the course of my nature—that he could never whip me into the obedience of his sphere without making me a monster?

I became a monster, I suppose, to satisfy him, but he could not hold me. I was not a good disciple.

"My poor mother," said Katie, and her hospital gown blew open like a sail in the dying wind. "She didn't have a lot of experience with psychiatry.

"Do you think it's a science, Izzy? I'm not sure. As far as I can tell, they don't even know what they're trying to study. Bones, brain, moonlight—they have no idea.

"Mom called in experts—expensive people—and I don't think they even saw my mind. There was my body, lying on a bed, and it wanted to die. So they thought they had me figured out. They thought for sure they knew what kind of sickness was in my mind. But I was ten miles above them, flying at the moon. I wasn't there, Izzy. I wasn't in my body. I hardly ever am any more."

What to do about Katie's gown? Surely she was not aware that her gown was open. Should I tell her so she could close it, or would she be happier if she never knew that she was naked for the world to see?

"Mom still doesn't know if she did the right thing. Her family didn't see psychiatrists; when they suffered it was called despair. You don't see a doctor for despair. But I was going to die, and I don't blame her. If I had cancer and she called in a witch doctor, that would be okay too. I mean, it would be no loss, and maybe it might help."

She was silent for a moment. "No loss, except dignity."

She started to cry again. Katie cried so often that you would think I'd have gotten used to it, but I never did. She never gave me neurotic tears; they were always real tears, real eyes. It was as hard for her to cry as anyone. She just had more reason.

"We were a dignified family, Izzy. I had integrity, as a little girl. I know that sounds stupid, but some little girls have integrity. Their body belongs to them, and they know it. Their mind belongs to them.

"Nothing belongs to me any more, Izzy. My mind is on record—everything I think, it's in a file on a shelf.

Any intern who wants to sleep with me and can't just has to look me up and read me wide open. Well, I might as well sleep with him, don't you think? You can fuck someone and give away less."

I decided not to tell her about her gown.

"But I don't blame my mother. Dignity isn't a medical thing, and it was a medical decision. Death is important. And I was going to die.

"I still don't know, however. If I'd cut my wrists, how much of me would I have lost? I wasn't in my body, you know: I was miles away, floating on a silver cord, staring down at those poor psychiatrists, who were all so much more lost than I was.

"They strapped me to a bed; they thought they had all of me strapped to this bed, and they moved me so gently, Izzy. It was funny, as if a little bump was going to make things worse."

Katie noticed that her gown was less than a strip of cloth, hiding nothing. She pulled it about her, wearily, but did not blush.

Then she asked me, with urgency and sincerity, "Do you like to look at me, Izzy? Am I still good to look at?"

Professor Abraham Gold seemed the precise antithesis of his predecessor. The search committee never did adequately account for their procedure, but it did not matter so much, because within a month the most stalwart Beachamite was effusively proclaiming the new doctrine.

I was a perfect target for Professor Gold. If you felt modernity had set you adrift, if you thought the quality of your love was not strong enough, if you had a sense of something too evil to be reasoned away, then Professor Gold would speak to you with words that you wanted to hear.

The Beachamites were of course in precisely this predicament.

It is difficult to pin down exactly what the doctrine offered. It was easy enough to determine what it *seemed* to offer, because this is what made it attractive. It seemed to make sense of lives that had been torn apart by questions; it seemed to provide a family to students whose families were broken; it seemed to make citizens of anarchists. The sense that you might belong—that you would belong, if you understood and agreed with Professor Gold—was too strong for the traumatized Beachamites to deny.

My experience was no different from anyone else's. When asked to describe the first lecture of Professor Gold's—the one that caught my interest and would not let it go—I found myself saying that he had somehow spoken about precisely what I wanted to hear; he had expressed a profound theoretical attraction to a problem I had thought was mine alone. The first time I sat in on Professor Gold's course, he was talking about memory.

"I'm not a philosophical person, Izzy. I'm not. Some people think all the time. It's what they do with their desire." Katie smiled. "I have other ways, I guess. Or I used to. But I started to think pretty hard when they put me in the hospital. I wanted to figure it out. I guess nobody had every done anything to me before that I didn't understand."

Katie started to read pornography. Pornography and Nietzsche. "When Nietzsche talks about women, it upsets me, but I want to listen. Somehow, when other men talk about women, I don't trust them—I'm sure they're lying. When men want nothing more than to seduce you, they lie . . .

"Nietzsche talks about the joy of rape. Did you know that, Izzy? He talks about a joy, a desire that men have, to rape women."

I became defensive. "Not all men—"

"All men. It's the way men are. Some men, the good ones, keep it all inside. They know this desire exists in them, but they refuse to feed it. Nietzsche, for instance—he did philosophy instead. But it was still there. The want. He said so.

"What kind of joy is that, Izzy? Where do you find joy in that?"

She was asking the question of me. Not of man in general, but of me. Because she knew, from reading Nietzsche, that the structure of my desire admitted this need, however I tried to push it into the shadows.

I can't tell you how much I wanted to protest. If I could find the logic, I would put this superstition to rest. If I could even say, with a degree of honesty: I don't feel that need, Katie, there's no joy in that for me.

But part of me bit back on my words, because I knew that there was a creature, a golden sharp beast called out by a singing electrode, and it was me, as much me as any, and it had desires whose nature I could only guess at. What had it done in the night while I slept, in my name, in the name of my wants and needs.

Katie was not accusing me. She had forgiven me, long before she asked the question. She had forgiven my entire sex, it seems, except for the visitor, the one who had given range to that desire as if it were some mere hunger, some passing want that had to be stayed by fulfillment.

"I started to read pornography, Izzy. It sounds silly, I know, but there's a key there, don't you think? If I could feel what men feel when they see those girls there, imprisoned in photos . . . I listen to pornography, and it says: rape me. Doesn't it? Rape me with your eyes. A boy can just open a book and take a woman, any time he wants her, without asking permission. She has an inviting smile on her face, and she can't take it off, no matter what he says to her, what he says he wants from her. It may not be rape, but it feeds the same desire. It's the same joy."

Katie smoked, calmly. "I wanted to feel that joy. Just to understand. Then maybe I could forgive him. That's what I thought. But I was wrong."

There was a collection of paperbacks on the ward. A sort of library. When you finished a book, you left it there. Somebody—I don't think it was a doctor—left a book called *The Story of the Eye.*

By now I had visited Katie more than once where she lived. I knew about her. Though her voice had been

154

back for some time, it could still disappear for hours. Often it was me. If I said something cruel, or even indifferent, Katie would lose the ability to answer, and I would suffer through her silence, taking back my words all the while.

She could surprise me. This day, as we met in the lobby of the hospital, she surprised me as I had never been surprised before.

Katie seemed annoyed. I had said nothing, except "Hello," but she was irritated. I should have taken it as a sign that she was not in her hospital gown; she had a long wine-colored dressing gown over a white shift, and she looked regal, especially in her censorious mood.

"Katie, what?"

"Don't ask me 'what'," she said, annoyed.

I was pained, and silent for a moment. When I spoke, I tried to force an element of reason into my voice. "I've never seen you like this."

"*You* have never seen me."

With this she walked away. She crossed the lobby, with straight and haughty shoulders, and she did not look back. I followed her. Meekly.

Katie turned down a narrow corridor and walked to the end. She opened a heavy door, and stood holding it. I caught up to her, and looked at the symbol above her hand: a generic stick figure in a skirt.

Katie took a step inside, still holding it open for me. I looked around, confused.

"In here," she said, and I stepped inside. It was an individual washroom, large and white, with two sinks and a toilet. "These are the only doors that lock."

"Why are you upset?" I asked.

"Shh." And she locked the door.

For a long time she stood facing me, her eyes sad and full of judgment, as if she had at last decided that I was mortal, or worse. Without taking her eyes off mine, she opened the knot in her wine-red belt and let the gown fall open, revealing the white shift, which came only to her thighs. Her legs were long and naked and turned inward slightly, as if she were cold, or being perversely modest. She leaned back against the wall and pulled the shift up to her stomach. I stared at the perfect isosceles triangle of white cotton with its apex between those moonbeams.

There was a vertical line at the apex, a soft indentation in the material, and I knew this was her sex, that from here was born all comfort and pain, and I wondered—odd that I wondered this—what she tasted like. Katie was still angry, still confident, but now slightly shy in the tilt of her head and the focus of her eyes. I could see that this thin long dimple, this simple indentation that was a sign of everything, was faintly damp. My breath sounded loud in my ears.

I kissed her so insistently that it took the breath out of her body, and when my hand came up to touch her breast through the cotton she made a sound as if she were going to cry, but I saw now, looking into her eyes, that she was not: it was a strange kind of pain that came into her eyes, a "what are you going to do to me" vulnerability, and she was quite happy to feel it. There were so many things I did not yet know.

She wrapped her legs around one of mine as if it were a tree, and climbed it, so that I could hear her breathing increase with the altitude. She pressed that damp patch of white cotton into me, feeling for the bone at the center of my flesh, and I moved my leg into her, rhythmically, with a rhythm I had learned at conception, and not once did she close those eggshell eyes, but stared into mine with increasing vulnerability until her mouth opened in a silent question and her eyebrows pulled together in an expression of hurt and she cried out with her whole body, cried out in a shudder that went right through her body and into mine, cried: *Take me out of this body I am so lonely.*

And my leg was wet where her sex had pressed against it. It was a point at which she might have succeeded, where her body might have flowed beyond its personal barrier into mine.

Feeling strong, I lifted her shift up high and began to kiss a line down the center of her body, slowly, to see whether she would stop me, kissed the hard spot between her breasts and then her soft inverted navel, kissed her where the cotton made a line between her hips, then peeled the damp white slowly back to reveal soft curls of bread-colored hair, and then, what I had never seen before, what I had thought in Katie would be eternally denied my kind, and what was astonishing in its simplicity—how can we desire so terribly something so simple?—a line in the soft flesh, which unfolds into a deeper color, the way the parched earth peels away beneath the plow to reveal a richer color, wet clay;

but here it was simply white flushing to a soft pink, though profoundly wet. I placed my tongue in the pink fold of her sex and kissed it as if it were a mouth.

"Decaying sense impressions." Professor Gold leaned forward into the broad desk—he always lectured sitting—and repeated these words. "Decaying sense impressions."

He leaned back and breathed heavily, as if these words tired him. Then he grasped the desk and spoke vigorously.

"I often wonder why my students have no sense of themselves; why they feel small and insubstantial; why they complain so bitterly. And though I have come up with many reasons over the years—all of them valid—I can say with certainty that the most serious flaw in your picture of yourselves is connected with this long discredited faculty: memory."

I was sitting in the front row, as I always did; I was an aggressive listener. Professor Gold seemed to flow over the desk. He was unusually animated for a man of his bulk and consistency. Though I had met him in the hall, and shaken his hand, I had never heard him speak before, and I was enthralled.

"Most of you, perhaps all of you, have this impoverished notion, which you have inherited from certain cowardly thinkers in the seventeenth century. Your memory, as far as you can tell, is no more than a faded picture of what your eyes have given you. It is a decayed image of your sensible lives. And the life of your senses, if I am not mistaken, is nothing particularly memorable to begin with.

"Because you have no adequate concept of memory—no theory whereby you might gain access, say, to something higher than the prison of your days, the tedium of your miserable particularity—you experience nothing internally but the slow death of your past experience.

"You look back over your life. What is it, this 'life,' except a creeping march of petty crimes, a stumbling dance of humiliating error, the revenge of your untutored passions? Am I right?

"What you call memory is simply this: images in fading sepia of—what?—women you have groped instinctively; perhaps men you have lain down before out of boredom or the need to be punished; in short, half-conscious couplings that you elevate to the status of love because that word has no meaning to you, in this time.

"What you miss, what you do not simply lack but in some sense actively miss, is a concept of memory that might take you out of this bleak terrain entirely, might lift you beyond the prisonyard of your senses, a faculty that might allow you to recapture something of worth.

"Though I know"—and here he laughed, with derisive pity—"that you do not suffer antique notions here—I know how sophisticated you are, in the wake of the great Profesor Beacham—I cannot help but mark how thin you are."

He laughed, and his body quivered on the broad desk like spilled gelatin.

"Not only thin and pale in body, like students out of Chekhov, but insubstantial in soul. Yes, yes, I know"— and he closed his eyes wearily—"that you do not have souls, not here, in this classroom. Professor Beacham has adequately banished the soul from discourse. It should not surprise you, then, if your soul does not exist, that it is somehow impoverished."

He opened his eyes and impaled me upon them. "I am not ambitious. I am not going to try to convince you, soulless sophisticate, that part of you is like a god, because you'll laugh at me." He narrowed his eyes; I shivered. "And that would not be appropriate."

"So I am going to concentrate on a faculty that you know you possess, however simple your concept of it may be. No, you do not have a soul—not yet—but . . ." He smiled, and I found myself smiling back, a fond idiot. "You have a memory."

Language hides the deep divisions. I would use the word "love" with Katie, and then the same word in the classroom, but I could not acknowledge until much later that they meant two very different things.

Love with Katie was strong and present, calling up senses I did not know I had. Primordial senses: I gained the sense of smell I associated with blind men and wolves. I learned the scent of Katie's hair. If you put out my eyes I would still know her hair from any other woman's. I would know that scent today, but it is gone.

I forgot about shame, and learned compassion. There may well be something called compassion that we know about before we are civilized. In that case I learned it again; I remembered. Whatever we did was hardly civilized—we made love on the floor of the washroom, because that was the only place there was—but we were, at least for a time, kinder to each other than most couples are in bed.

I learned Katie's life, and it became as much my history as my own. I wanted to know why she had cried at age four when her mother was sick; how she had learned to read and think; every change and color in her personal story, which was five years longer than mine. I was turning seventeen and Katie was twenty-two, but I became older to meet her; I took in her years and made them mine.

Increasingly, however, I was aware of Professor Gold. He did not hold the sense of smell in high esteem. Compassion for him was a form of unwitting hypocrisy: a tender lie for weaker men. The memories of a young woman—her daily life—had almost nothing to do with what he called memory. And the idea of a boy, a busboy in the cafeteria, making love to a mental patient on the floor of a washroom would be perhaps as repugnant to Professor Gold as any scenario he could possibly invent. I knew this.

I talked about love, and I made love, and another rift opened in my life, as my words no longer made sense of my actions.

Katie's ward was entirely without ornament. The windows had no frames, the walls no moldings. Nothing protruded to hang your body from; nothing intruded to catch your desire. It was clean and white, and the abiding smell was an acidic component they used on the walls to discourage unwelcome forms of life.

They were two to a room, and her roommate was a good person. She had been an opera lover, and in her two years at the hospital she might have escaped despair had she been permitted, even once, to go to the opera house, where the opera wasn't even very good. But they had not allowed her to, so she whistled about in a permanent fugue and became less than a person. She drank Katie's urine sample the first night, and Katie could not sleep for the retching.

Yet it was for the most part an unimpeachable environment.

Katie read Bataille. She sympathized with the great pornographer; she believed that the decadence was simply a means to a more dignified end, an overcoming of the self. She read the entire book, an orgy of urine and blood, trying always to keep it in perspective: she endured it because she hoped, like Bataille, that the road through horror was the last path towards the divine.

The great fluorescents dimmed to black as she read, and the walls grew shadows in areas where shadows could not grow; the gargoyles pushed their hidden faces from the flat surfaces and the windows bent into pointed arches.

The nurses grew transparent—they were never far from transparent—until they were wraithlike, gibbering. She might not even have noticed them if it were not for the pity that naturally arose in her whenever they moved through her, making their small noises. Katie was a well of pity.

She felt there was intrigue where there had been none, that there was a dark current where there had been no river, that all of the science flowered through the shit in Bataille until it once again murmured something, almost impossible to hear, about the human soul.

She hung her sheets out the window on white nights so they would catch the moonlight; they said truce, I surrender, come into the black quadrangle my brutal tormentor and we will talk. Heal me.

The sheets hung from the bars beneath the arch, white flags, milk in rectangular saucers. Come, feline.

And one night, black with Bataille, when the moon was like a bucket of milk, she heard soft paws padding about in the quadrangle. They were silent, but she heard them, just as she could feel the sharpness of the claws retracted into their place. Her heart sickened green in her chest, but she leaned out between the bars and called.

The low growl that answered sent deep vibrations through the bars; the gargoyles' stone teeth chattered; the shadows jumped and then bowed low to their master. I have come.

And in that moment of sound, so low that she had to press against the bars to feel it, Katie knew that what she had called up was no familiar, it was the rending between her legs, it was not her species, not her friend and never would be, she would never be reconciled.

"No!" she cried. "I didn't mean to invite you . . . Leave me . . . Leave me alone, please, I hate you!"

This would not have meant much, except Katie had never hated anything before, and it crippled some necessary part of her to do so now.

The creature, almost golden in the moonlight, slouched away.

There were machines at the hospital too subtle to be understood. Machines on Katie's floor. She knew nothing about them; the doctors, in fact, knew nothing about them, except that they were effective. They cured misery. They cured misery, the way death cured misery: they cut a great swath across the conscious mind and left in its place nothing.

Katie stumbled into the cafeteria in a hospital gown, stamped and wrinkled, her face as pale as any nurse's. I had never seen her without color. She shuffled in and sat down, and stared off at the wall.

"Katie?"

She looked at me with a questioning smile, as if she were surprised to hear her name. "Yes . . ."

"Are you okay?"

"Yes, I think so. Yes . . ." She frowned. "Do I know you?"

I cannot say what would have been an appropriate reaction, but I laughed. I laughed the way an audience will when the action on stage becomes too horrible to watch, in order to break the tension, to express disbelief, in hopes that everyone including the players will join in, begin laughing, and that all will be well again. But Katie did not laugh. She stood.

"I'm sorry, I think you have the wrong person." She began to edge away, and I touched her hand.

"Katie. You're making me nervous."

Perhaps something in my touch conveyed an honest confusion, because she sat down again. She examined my face. I could see her eyes move, change focus, as if my face were a map and she were trying to find her bearings.

"How long have I known you?"

"Stop this!"

"How long?"

"Some months. A few. I don't know . . . Come on, Katie, a joke's a joke."

She smiled. "A month? That explains it."

"Explains what? What's to explain?"

"I'm being treated."

"Yes, so what?"

"A new treatment. I'm sorry—don't be insulted—it's doing funny things to my memory. I don't remember the past months that well." She paused. "In fact, I don't remember them at all."

"At all . . ."

"So I'm sorry, I mean . . . if I know you . . . and I guess I do . . . but I just don't remember."

I stood this time. I was going to leave. If she had told me that she had died in her sleep—"I'm sorry, Izzy, I am no longer alive"—it would have been less strange, perhaps easier to take in.

"The doctor said it was unusual, losing this much time.

165

Usually the treatment takes out a day or so, sometimes a week."

"And when does it all come back?" My voice was small.
She shrugged, again smiling. "It might not."

I began to walk away. She followed, but I could not be with her. I was angry, I discovered, and I had a right to be angry, but not with Katie. What I had lost, she had lost as well. I briefly hated her for allowing it to happen, for letting it slip away, be cut away—whatever she had allowed them to do to us.

"Stop. I'm sorry. What's your name? Please stop."

I stopped but I did not turn. She touched my neck, and I shut my eyes, so tightly that I could hear the skin tighten around my ears.

"I guess I know you pretty well. Is that it?"

"It's only been a couple of months."

"But I know you."

"You know me as well as . . . people can know each other in that kind of time."

I looked at her face, and she dropped her eyes.

"This isn't treatment, Katie. You're not being cured."

"The doctors said it wouldn't harm me."

"What? What wouldn't harm you? What is it they're doing?"

"It's just an electric shock. Makes you go into . . . I don't know, a seizure or something."

"Katie!"

She put her white hands to her mouth. "Were we lovers?"

Katie sat on the nearest chair, very still for a moment, then began rocking back and forth. "Were we lovers?"

"I don't know. I thought so. I don't know."

She rocked in silence for a moment.

"But we were."

"I don't know."

"Tell me."

"You don't even know my name!"

She put her fingers to my lips. She was crying.

"Look, Katie. We're not lovers. Maybe we were, but we aren't now. Some things only make sense if they're continuous. If there's no story, nothing you can tell yourself, no story about how we met, when we decided that it meant something, how it all changed . . . You have to remember some of that—at least some of it—and you don't. We don't have a story."

Katie had begun to smile. And then she kissed me. It must have been hard for her, an immense suspension of disbelief, to kiss a complete stranger as if she were in love with him.

"We still have a story," she said, still smiling. "Tell me."

And there on the plastic chairs I narrated for the first time the story between us. I have told it since. I am telling it now. Parts of it must have been told in a way that pleased her, because she listened with growing amusement, brushed her tears off on her wrist, laughed even, and by the end was prepared to want me as she had before.

I was astounded that she trusted me as she did.

Imagine what I might have told her. The responsibility was terrible, but for the first time I felt I bore it well. I tried to tell her the truth.

It was an important discovery, the uneasy comfort of that kind of activity. I often return to it when lost: the desperate attempt to reconstitute the past in words that do not lie. It is like building a house.

I made her promise that she would never again allow them to do that to her mind. It was, unfortunately, a promise she could not keep. They showed her a release form, and though she could not remember signing it, her signature flowed across a corner in black ink. She had given her permission and could not take it back.

Professor Gold spread his hands, wearily, and the folds between them stretched out thinly, translucent webbing. "You make too much of this pale world. You are at an age where your passions are strong, but without guidance. You are beguiled by your senses, enthralled by what you consider real."

He scratched at the surface of his desk with a long nail, disgusted by the facticity of the wood. "En-thralled. A thrall is a slave, and you are slaves.

"What can I possibly offer you to compete with this? How can I hope to seduce you? I am an old man, and all I have are books and words. The most foolish young girl is better armed than I am to steal your affections, strip you down until you are less than a beast, and own you completely.

"How am I supposed to turn your eyes up from the earth? Even the physical sciences conspire against me.

I sit here, alone trying to convince you that the world has a higher order, that there is an order to the cosmos that is sublime and beautiful, that the apprehension of this order, through the faculty of memory, is the purest imaginable joy." He closed his eyes, deeply pained, and we felt for him. "And immediately upon leaving the room it is all undone by one of my helpful colleagues. Your next class is some miserable affair in a white laboratory, where you torture matter until it confesses: I am shallow, and cold, and mean nothing to you.

"No doubt this confuses you. These men in their white lab coats, unlike me, have the utmost credibility. They are purveyors of all that is most true and good, the highest rational principles in an age of science: physical laws. Yet they are somehow not very seductive. The cold lump of matter in the laboratory never says anything that you truly want to hear, and if it did, you would suspect your senses of lying.

"So. You see the difficulty of my position. Why should you wish to be wise when the only form of wisdom you know is without joy, cold and mundane? Of course you prefer to fornicate like beasts in the mud, where there is at least some joy. The cost is nothing: what do you care for your dignity?

"I am fighting a lonely battle. I am obsolete, and superstitious." Professor Gold gazed about the room, his eyes like searchlights, to satisfy himself that we were all shaking our heads vigorously: no, not all all, sir.

"But I am an educator. That is my burden. It is my curse to stumble about the university, a comical figure, ranting on in antiquated language about a rare faculty,

169

something each of you possesses, however stunted, a means by which the sublime order of the universe can be made accessible. Though everything has been forgotten, and we are quite satisfied in the mud, I shall continue to stress the importance of memory. However absurd you think me. It will be easy enough for you to deny me. Keep that earnest look on your face; take notes and write a flattering exam. It will be easy enough to laugh secretly at what I am saying and yet pass this course."

He looked up, again, with a contemptuous smile. "Deny me, however, and you will remain less than human."

"I can't even read!"

Three times now Katie had stumbled into the cafeteria, each time more distracted than the last, and three times I told the story of how we had met, and who I was, and what I meant to her. She was changing, however. The treatment was diffusing her, splitting her focus, fragmenting her self. To an extent it was successful. Because she no longer remembered why she was without hope, the despair mattered less, and because the edges of her mind were now crumbling away like old bread, the brute fact of her pain lost its edge. Her complaint, now, was mundane: she couldn't get things done.

"I can't read at all. I can't keep a whole sentence in my mind. I find myself staring at the same word for hours, and it doesn't mean anything."

Katie frowned. "Whole books are gone. I used to read good books. They changed me. I had whole books in my mind, and thoughts about those books. My world was changed because of those books—I'm sure of it—and now they're gone. I don't remember. I can't read. I don't know who I am . . . I don't know who I am . . ."

She smoked with a new compulsive intensity, crushing the end of the cigarette between her nervous fingers and pulling air through it as if that were the air she breathed. She lit one cigarette off the other so that her head was never clear of its halo of gray.

We still clutched each other on the floor of the women's washroom, but it was different now: Katie did not know me. I was anonymous, a man she had only just met in the lobby, and though she believed me each time I told her that we had a history, she made hungry, craving love to me as if it were an addiction: necessary, smoke.

Why did I begin to pull away? Certainly she needed me now more than she ever had before: I was all that kept her days from pulling apart into flashes and segments; I was her memory. Why then was this revulsion setting in? I had always wanted nothing more than to mean everything to Katie, and now that was literally true: without me to reconstruct the continuity of her life, there was no meaning.

My only explanation is theoretical, abstract, perhaps wrong. I was beginning, just beginning, to overcome my weakness, and it was crucial that I develop a strong attitude towards it. The reformed alcoholic, for instance: he does not merely dislike alcohol—he reviles it, he loathes it, he allows it to stand for all the world's misery, and he rejects it utterly.

There is no excuse for what I did to Katie. But her current misery was the weakness I had to overcome in myself. I too once had trouble reading. Now that I could read again—now that I was learning about memory— Katie began to stand for everything I associated with the most oppressive period in my life. Never mind that she was the one who had pulled me out. I could not abide her.

The last machine that Aaron built, before he left home, ensured that he would never return. This last machine arranged it so that there was no home to return to.

I don't know what it was supposed to do. It was a project, his first project in Engineering Science, and perhaps he had some sense from the start that it would bring into focus the growing violence between my mother and my father. My mother now spent most of her time either away and wandering or holed up in Josh's room, reading. My father had become eloquent in his protest; he had become frail, and human, and though he built cities and was respected for it, he could do nothing with his own family but lament the growing ruination.

The machine Aaron was building now was heavy. He had to reinforce the walls of the house with trusswork, flying buttresses, huge beams of treated wood that made powerful triangles in the backyard. He convinced my father that they were temporary, which they in fact were, but only because there was little to support when the experiment was finished.

Aaron, it seems, had become interested in the machinery of medicine. There was a lot of money to be made in the field. He was specifically interested in the human mind: how it could be modeled on a computer, scanned and monitored and made to produce an image of itself in electrical pictures. I gather that his machine did something like this. It scanned the house, determined the affective state of the occupants, and reproduced that state in real space, as physical phenomena.

When my father despaired in the garden, the machine sent shivers through the walls. When my mother came home from one of her week-long disappearances, and shut herself into Josh's room without even saying hello, a window in Aaron's room melted. It was ominous, this emotional echo, but none of us truly comprehended the nature of that machine until our own thoughts moved it to demonstrate its full capacity. Even Aaron was surprised, I think: he knew what his machine was capable of, but never imagined that his own family could produce that kind of inspiration.

Our awe for the power of machines, our almost superstitious regard for the technological, is really a form of hidden narcissism. It is helpful for us to believe that a machine could some day become fully human, or at least adequately mirror the complete depth of the human self, because this particular article of faith grants potential autonomy to our creations, and further succeeds in masking our vanity. Look: they deserve our worship, and they are utterly independent of us. The psychological truth is less palatable. We adore the potential of our machinery because it is considered vulgar to worship that potential in man.

I was pleased that my brother had developed, at least subconsciously, a profound sense of irony. His machine was more obviously an expression of this hidden narcissism that most: it was entirely dependent, and offered us nothing but images of ourselves magnified. It was merely the symptom, and we could turn nowhere but inward to find the disease.

It was fitting that the house should collapse over dinner. Drama was beginning to make sense to me, and meals provide the critical environment for drama in the family. These shared rituals are when the relations of dependence become most obvious and the strains in those relations most clear. Who cooks? Who buys the food? Whose money buys the food? Who eats, and how? With what kind of arrogant neglect does a family member eat? With how little awareness of who cooks, whose money buys the food? . . .

Except in matters of food and shelter, no member of my family shared with any other a common purpose. The house was our theater, and the dinner table our sole prop.

My mother cooked, that night, for the first time in months. She did not cook lamb. She made brisket, made it well; there was nothing to fault in the meal. And that was a problem.

My father was prepared for a confrontation. This becomes obvious in retrospect. He fully expected some aspect of the meal to fuel a legitimate controversy, which he could fan into a bright spark. It was necessary that he go off, like the loaded gun on stage, yet my mother provided no just cause. I can see now that had she done so, the damage might have been contained and focused. As it was, like a gun with a plugged barrel, my father had to explode.

"Pass the potatoes," he said. And then: "My son is dead."

Nobody passed the potatoes.

"My son is dead, and my wife is wandering the streets, my streets—I built those streets—wandering like some woman dispossessed. We are eating brisket. Many families eat brisket. How many families eat brisket, however, like this? With death and silence and wandering . . . This for a family? I have no youngest son."

This hurt me.

"I have no wife. I have no family. I work, and I pay, and the money that I pay means that we can have brisket, but I could pay this money from far away, and nothing would change. You would still wander and die and be silent and strange and I would have no family."

My mother began to cry. Full, bitter tears, as she had never shed when Josh died. She was lamenting something, keening almost, but my father did not stop talking.

"Pass the salt," he said. "My son is dead."

Nobody passed the salt.

"I do not have a conversation with anyone in this house. I talk easily. I do. Freely. My colleagues tell me

this: I'm an approachable guy. But this is my house—
my house!—and you look at me as if I have nothing to
say. And you . . . you have nothing to say to me. My
family has nothing to say to me."

My father reached across the table and put his large
hand around the saltshaker. He did not salt anything;
he simply held it in his fist and stared at it.

"I believe in the family. You may not, but I believe
in the family. I was raised to believe in the family. I
was told that you give to the family . . . that you expect nothing in return. That is . . . a responsibility. So
I will give. I will continue to give. But I cannot live in
this house if I can't even get a conversation—just some
talk—in return for what I give. I'll give from . . . far
away. No strings. You don't have to talk to me, when I
am far away. It won't matter that you say nothing to
me, and that I say nothing to you."

Through my mother's sobs, we could hear the begin-
nings of a noise in the far corner of the house. It was a
scraping noise, steel on glass, the kind of noise that ter-
rifies out of all proportion with its volume. And it was
getting louder. My father turned the shaker over in his
hand, slowly, and salt began to pour out on the table.
We all sat in silence, watching the salt form a cone on
the surface of the table. When the shaker was empty,
my father put it in his pocket.

"I have no right to do what I am going to do. I am
going to leave you, and I am not going to return."

My mother covered her face in her hands, but my
father pulled her hands down and held them in his own.

"I don't love you any more," he said. And then, loudly,

176

so loudly that the splitting of the house was briefly drowned in my father's voice, he screamed: "You cannot be loved!"

The house split where the partition wall had always stood. Once a duplex, it became two houses for a moment, in violent memory of its origins, then the two halves caved in upon themselves without the structural support of the whole. Some rooms remained intact. The kitchen and dining room were unharmed, and Josh's room miraculously survived, the only unbroken space on the second floor. Aaron's machine, which had spoken only as eloquently as my father, whose decision it made flesh, was destroyed in the fire that swept the third floor. My room no longer existed. This was almost a relief. It had never belonged to me. I had always known it might be taken away, and now it was gone.

I continued to attend lectures at the university. Professor Gold did not have time for students from broken homes, however; he was convinced that my potential had been ruined. He expected total blind allegiance from his students, and those from broken homes were never again capable of that kind of trust. Even the most solid relations between people were subject to examination, and this did not suit Professor Gold at all.

There was always some truth to what the professor said, and I did in fact become a skeptic. I allowed myself certain luxurious hypotheses: What if Professor Gold were, in essence, a liar? A seducer? What if he did not believe his own incredible doctrine? What if, as in his predecessor, there were some horrible emptiness at the core which would out, if not in his own steeled life, in the life of his credulous students? What if, in the choice between Katie and Professor Gold, I was turning from the real and embracing a cold fiction?

In a sense I was lucky: I saw through Professor Gold quite early. Too late for Katie, but before I had been made over entirely in the shape of a lie.

Professor Gold: There is much that you will have to reject. If there is perfection in the order of the world, and if you can be educated to remember this perfection, it will only be at some cost. I know what you love. It will have to go.

"Katie?" She was so thin now, and her eyes were red from the smoke she moved through, but she was still Katie, beautiful in the way she would always be because I knew her. "Katie?" There is no moment's beauty in those whom we have loved for a long time. We do not admire them, the way we do some chance woman or man on the subway, as a moment's appearance of perfection in the physique. We see them as a montage of every remembered moment, the present one often more vivid and strong than those receding into the past, but a montage nevertheless. If we remember.

Professor Gold: You are governed by passions, often the most destructive passions. I am not fooled by your faces, all attention and bright hypocrisy. I see you for what you are.

Izzy: If we remember. But we can easily forget. In the immediacy of some crisis . . . including passion . . . we can easily forget all of those other moments, and despite our history with someone, they and their personal beauty can collapse into a present singularity. And the content of that present moment—lust, revulsion, indifference—the content of that changing moment becomes everything we know.

Watching Katie there, I allowed myself to forget. I made myself forget. She was thin, with prominent veins in her eyes, and she was smoking in her hospital gown like one of those women without sex who people the cafeteria, and I forced myself to forget.

Professor Gold: I know what you love. I can feel the powerful confusion behind your composed features; I can hear your questions: What does it taste like? What?

Izzy: I made her into a moment's woman. I forgot that she had told me about her first lover, about the books that she had read, about her family and her integrity as a little girl.

Professor Gold: You do not read about rape without putting yourself into the soul of the rapist. I can hear your questions: if I had been there, and the circumstances the same, would I have done the same thing? What separates me, you wonder, from the monsters of history? Anything?

Izzy: I was capable of . . . rejecting this woman.

Professor Gold: As yet, nothing does. There is no qualitative difference. I know what you love. You are betrayed by your passions, and should the circumstances arise, you will be utterly betrayed.

Izzy: There is a point at which love becomes a burden. If you love me and I cannot return that love, then I may find myself reacting not simply with indifference but with cruelty. You will have become a burden, and I will have to send you away.

Professor Gold: There is, however, one passion that leads beyond itself, that gives birth to a state more pure than the dubious circumstance of its begetting: and this is the love between the educator and his pupil. It is the means by which the memory is teased out. It is the love that forgets its carnal origins, and does service to the Beautiful.

"Katie, I can't go on."

I become tongue-tied and strange when what I have to say amounts to a crime. I clutch at banalities, knowing that no matter how insipid my words, the vicious import cannot be drained away.

"You can't go on?"

"It's hard to explain." It was. To be honest, I never properly did. I said no more than most men have said when they felt it necessary to extricate themselves from a situation; I used surprisingly ordinary words.

"We're going in separate directions. Can't you feel it? I'm at this point . . . I'm learning something, for the first time. I feel like I'm growing, as if any day now it's all going to make sense. And you . . ."

"What about me?"

The treatments were finished. Again I had done my best to restore Katie's knowledge of who we were, but this time I did it hollowly, because I was no longer sure that I was convinced. I was initiating her into a love that for me was already mostly forgotten. She took my story from me like food. She wanted me in a way that made me almost sick; it seemed carnal, pure body, like the function of the stomach, like the craving of the lower intestine. I wanted something more.

"What about me?" she asked again.

I could only say what I was about to say, because I was convinced that I was purging a lie: the lie of the senses, the lie that told me I loved some mere creature, that I could love her no matter how dire the circumstances. I was convinced that I was purging a lie to embrace the truth.

"The world is a brutal place. Some of the facts of this world are . . . brutal. When two . . . friends . . . change fortunes, so that one of them is rising while the other is falling, then it is a . . . fact that they pull apart."

One of the side effects of the treatment was an occasional nervous tic, an involuntary pulling at the side of Katie's lip, which repelled me. Her lip was now quivering, a spastic movement; I had seen old women quiver like this after a stroke. Katie was becoming old. They had made her old at twenty-two, had ruined her, mind and body.

"Izzy, what about me?"

"I should never have told you about us. I should have let you forget. It was a mistake. It could have been painless, if you had never been told who I was."

Katie stood, now bloodless and trembling. She took a step backwards and tripped against a chair. While holding the edge of the table to keep herself from falling, she said: "I know you. I remember who you are."

"It's only because I've tried to be honest. I've been too honest."

"No. I know you."

Her voice had changed. There was horror in her voice, and though I knew I was being efficient, brutal even, I could not see that what I was saying merited this kind of terror, this degree of revulsion.

"I know you!"

"Katie . . ."

"You came to my room and gave me torn green pieces. You gave me roots, and a stem, and a leaf with red veins. You tore me open and left me lying in the wet of my own blood. You were golden and feline and I gave you my hospitality because I thought you loved me."

I heard what she was saying, but I did not believe her. I had felt something split from me in the ravine; I knew that crimes were being committed in my name; I was fully aware of the source of Katie's despair—her story—but I could not muster the resolve to do what I had to do if I believed what she was saying, so I did not.

What I had to do was leave her. It was not easy. Twice I came back, fucked her on the white tiles of the washroom on the first floor, because it was hard to pull away from so much comfort, however decayed. But finally I became strong. The words of Professor Gold made me strong. I conquered my need for Katie. I forgot her, and in my forgetting, overcame her. I left her.

Izzy Darlow, this small confessional monster, sat smoking in my office, his cigarettes pouring dust into my air, smoking and confessing as if I were in a position to forgive him, as if I would even be inclined to forgive him if it were in my power to do so.

He was now silent, having told me this last piece of the story. I was to have been married hours ago, and I could barely breathe. Over the course of his story—it was to be expected—I had fallen in love with Katie. I could see her; I had spoken to her; I felt that I had made love to her. And now this. Who did he think he was, that he could tell me this and expect forgiveness?

"You're a coward," I said, and he flinched. "That's what you want, isn't it? You want me to tell you what I think. I think you're a coward."

He bowed his head. "Don't judge me too harshly."

"That would be difficult. Where's Katie now?"

"I don't know."

"You never tried to find out? You just left her, in that state, because it suited you? You couldn't care less what you might have done to her."

"I cared. I just didn't know what to do."

"I think you should leave my office."

"Maybe I haven't explained properly . . ."

"Get out of my office!"

He was already standing; he had perhaps expected he would be asked to leave. One last time, however, those thieflike eyes shot upwards to find mine, to arrest me; I felt momentarily like an accomplice, and a wave of terrible guilt washed over me.

Then Izzy Darlow slouched out of my office, his story over but by no means complete. I put my head against my desk, listening to the silent wood, and wept for a woman I had never met.

4

*C*ITY

*The breakup of familiar order transposes whole peoples into a
sort of lifelong Toronto.*

Hugh Kenner

HE WALKS, BENT WITH KNOWLEDGE, through the door
of the Archive and into the wet trees of his new life.
Nobody sees him. He was going to be married, this
man who cannot stand straight, but that was hours ago.
He is not going to be married now.

The trees are wet with questions. Who is he? Where
does he come from? The rain wants to know. The leaves
cling to his feet in death, and the city crawls about him,
infested with itself, alive with the new life that a corpse
draws from the air.

He walks. Where will he go now? He cannot return
to his life. She gave him all of the life that he knew,
and he has left her standing, unmarried, somewhere in
the city. Where will the street take him?

This revulsion is new. To hate the city, he knows, is a species of self-loathing, and he finds that he hates it now. These buildings are alike, horribly alike, and without ornament. Men come to this city to go blind, and die.

A small boy appears, bleeding. The rain washes the blood away from his forehead, but there is always more blood, pushing through the skin. How much can he bleed, thinks the man, before his blood is all gone?

Can I tell you a story, says the boy.

You're bleeding.

Let me tell you my story.

The boy walks away, his blood finding its way in streams to the leaves in the gutter, and begins to tell his story. The man rushes behind, to catch the words before they are washed away in the rain.

Simonides the poet spoke with a lisp, a speech impediment that ought to have precluded any consideration of a career in rhetoric. He never made an attempt to overcome this liability; he never thought to place stones in his mouth in an effort to become more eloquent than the sea. Certainly, he did not achieve the fame of Demosthenes, at least not as a speaker, but he spoke well enough to be hired to banquets, and it was in this capacity that he achieved fame in a more arcane branch of rhetoric: he became the Father of Memory.

I used to have a lisp, says the boy.

Yes, and what happened?

I learned to sing.

I have been staring into a sleeping world, and it is coming awake. Something is awakening before my eyes. I cannot be married, not with everything changing as it is.

Shall I continue my story, says the boy.

Please.

The banquet table was laden with a progression of suckling pigs. Five piglets, in ascending size, beginning with the anthony, the runt of the litter. (St. Anthony would one day become the patron saint of pigs.) Then the mother, still glistening with the fat in which she had been roasted, her mouth stained with pomegranate. And then, seated at the head of the progression and licking grease from an iron fork, the host of the banquet: an obese creature with jowls.

"How am I to eulogize this monster?" thought Simonides, who as usual had not prepared for the occasion.

Simonides always spoke extemporaneously. Not by nature gifted with a divine memory, he found it laborious to memorize an entire speech. Sometimes this worked in his favor: his orations were thought lively and natural. But sometimes he found himself with too little material towards the middle of the speech, and for this reason he was becoming notorious for the introduction of strange and apparently inappropriate matters. Usually, however, he would succeed in making these peculiar subjects relevant through various gymnastic twists in logic. Simonides was, in fact, becoming famous for his concluding remarks. The drama was always palpable, the audience nervously leaning forward, wondering if the idiosyncratic poet would succeed in rendering the disparate elements of his oration into a convincing whole.

Once, when he succeeded in doing so against the most remarkable odds, the audience rose as a mass and carried the nerve-shot poet through the streets of the city, exclaiming loudly: "He has done it! Simonides has successfully discussed the breeding of goats in the midst of a funeral oration!"

Do you understand the stories that you tell?

No, says the boy. The voices come through me, and I am too young to make sense of them.

The man smiles, a grim smile: yes.

On the morning of the banquet, when he ought to have been preparing his eulogy, for which he was to be handsomely paid, Simonides consorted (on credit) with the famous twin prostitutes from Monaco: delicious fifteen-year-old boys, alike in every conceivable respect, except that one had an erection that curved slightly to the left, and the other to the right.

Simonides had sodomized both, and had found, on reflection, that he preferred a leftward-curving penis, as it fitted more easily into his dominant hand.

Where are you taking me?

To a place.

What place?

You'll see.

The man stands still for a moment, briefly stubborn: Why should I follow you? he thinks. The rain has come through the leather in his shoes.

What place?

The boy frowns beneath the blood on his forehead, impatient.

To school. Come on.

The introduction went without major difficulties. These encomia are formulaic: anyone, no matter how vile, can be praised for vague civic virtues, qualities of character, etc. The meat of the speech, however, was problematic. Simonides found it difficult not to dwell on a certain image: the succession of pigs, now reduced to skeletal remains. Every metaphor that came to mind was dangerously pastoral, and tending towards the porcine.

Simonides fell silent. He had almost said, quite without intending it: "Thus, we can see that there is little difference between our patron and this gorgeous sow."

He had intended to draw out the comparison, of course—how both were instrumental in the contentment of the revelers, how both had satiated the audience—but the sentence would have been disastrous.

At these moments, the mind relies upon cues, inner promptings. Give me an acceptable image, Simonides begged his feverish mind, and I shall elaborate upon it. He knew that he had until the conclusion, some fifteen minutes away, before he had to tie the image into the more general subject of the speech. Nothing would come, however, except a succession of inappropriate beasts: hogs, warthogs, bushpigs, hippopotamoi.

He gestured dramatically with his left hand—the

dominant one, the one that would rise naturally when he had to punctuate a particularly bombastic section of the speech, but nothing dramatic would out.

He closed his hand.

And then, almost palpably, Simonides felt in his hand, as if it were still morning, the leftward curve of the first twin's youthful erection. The poet's eyes shone. He looked up to the sky, prepared to intone a grateful prayer to whichever god first came to mind, for here was a note of inspiration.

The first constellation to catch his eye was Gemini, the Twins, and Simonides found himself progressing naturally from an eloquent defense of youth—always a popular topic—to a specific appreciation of Castor and Pollux, the youthful twin gods (to whom he felt particularly grateful, not only for saving his imperiled speech but for presiding over his morning's raptures).

The conclusion, he felt, was adequate: neither flawless, nor entirely farfetched. His host, however, was a crafty man, and parsimonious to a fault.

"I note," said the bulbous host, still licking his iron fork, "that you spent only half of your speech on the specific virtues pertaining to my person. Therefore, my good Simonides, I am prepared to pay you half of the sum agreed upon. The rest . . ." He chortled, with a generous appreciation of his own wit, "The rest you may collect from Castor and Pollux, as you have sung their praises with great eloquence."

The boy lapses into silence and the rain becomes loud. He stands staring up at a building with a sad smile of recognition, as if it were, at one time, a place that

189

made him happy. The man stands in the gutter beside him.

This is the school?

Yes.

Do you go to this school?

I did once.

Are you going to take me inside?

No. I'm going to stay here. You're going to take the stairs to the second floor.

I am? Why?

Because there's a library.

The party had repaired to an interior hall. As the flute girls were being led out for a third time, the naked butler entered and whispered something in the ear of the host. The host leaned forward, his womanish breasts sliding across the greased table, and addressed Simonides.

"Smile, my good poet. There are twin young men at the door, I am told, and they ask for you."

Simonides blushed, and the revelers laughed; all were aware, of course, of the twin prostitutes from Monaco who had created such a sensation since arriving in the capital.

"Do invite them in, Simonides. I am sure we can find entertainments to suit them."

Accompanied by the butler, and to the echo of jeers and merriment, Simonides made his way to the front door. He stepped outside into the night, which was lit like noon by the whirling stars.

There were no boys.

He turned towards the house. The butler had slipped inside. He was alone.

Simonides took a small step back towards the door, then hesitated; he felt two small hands take him by either elbow, and he looked about. But he was still alone.

There was a sound like the rending of bones. Simonides stumbled backwards as twin cracks appeared in the caryatids to either side of the portico. The pillars, carved in the form of women, split from their breasts to their navels as if to give monstrous birth. The portico shivered once, then the entire house collapsed inward on itself, the roof falling in a single slab and cracking only once, down the very center, when it met the floor.

Amongst the many screams, Simonides discerned one that he felt sure must be the dying squeal of his host, so much did it resemble a pig stuck on an iron fork.

Looking up at the sky, the poet fixed upon the twins, Castor and Pollux, who shone more brightly than he had ever seen them shine. They shone like eyes, laughing, in the broad face of the night.

Simonides fell slowly to his knees, trembling with awe, moving his mouth for a full minute without sound. And when the sound at last came, in a dry whisper, it was a hymn of praise. He gave eloquent and heartfelt thanks to the immortal twins, who had paid him so handsomely for his speech.

The man stands in the library, his clothes bleeding water onto the floor. The desks are too small; they are for people much smaller than he is.

He hears his own voice, tiny, inside his head. Then he hears the boy's story, also inside his head. He sits on one of the desks and puts his hands to his ears. A third voice intervenes.

"For a long time," says Izzy, in a voice some hours distant, "perhaps a week, I roamed the library undisturbed. I found a book on airplanes, which permitted me a view beneath the skin. I discovered that the most simple plane can have the most impossible skeleton, and that planes have internal organs much as we do. Birds' guts were next, and cutaway diagrams of birds' eggs, in which the center was not breakfastlike at all, but an actual bird. Only later would I discover those remarkable eggs from the Gobi desert: elliptical eggs, frozen in stone before they could give birth to three-story lizards."

All of the stories feeding into my life are fragmenting the integrity of my voice; I hear myself telling other people's stories as if they were my own, and I feel certain that there are people out there, people I hardly know, telling mine. I am a confluence of stolen narratives, and my own story has been stolen too and fed through a foreign mouth into foreign ears.

Simonides was called upon to identify the remains. The roof had crushed the banqueting guests and mutilated them beyond recognition, but they had to be identified if they were to be buried properly. The widows besieged the poet with sucking noises, pawing at his robe: "Must we bury our husbands in a mass grave, unnamed, like beggars after the plague?"

Some of the city's most illustrious citizens had been

at the banquet, and this raised also the appalling possibility that the wrong body would be eulogized.

Each had been crushed in his seat. Simonides wandered, sick, through the pulped remains, but all men look alike when their form is taken away by violence. They are like copper pots, thought Simonides, each battered into a separate lump of undifferentiated matter. How am I to tell them apart?

Of one body, however, he was certain. The one at the head of the table, of course, was the host. The crushed flesh would have been identifiable from its place at the table, even if it had not been impaled upon a bent fork. Simonides closed his eyes and called up a picture of the piglike man.

And with this thought, the art of memory was born.

An old man sits beside him, on a small desk. As he sits, his shoulders push up beside his neck, like the folded wings of a bat.

Izzy's voice, somewhere, continues: "I returned to the library last year for the first time, hoping to rediscover that early sense of place, but I was disappointed. The room was banal. Horribly banal. It was composed of public school bricks: great blocks of concrete desperately made cheerful by a coat of shiny paint. Rows of fluorescent tubes hung from the ceiling in louvered fixtures.

"Fluorescent light sickens me now. This is not a matter of taste, but an involuntary physical reaction. I can no longer read beneath lights that flicker, because a voice at my left shoulder whispers, 'The sun is failing; the sun is going out.' I do not feel at ease with a color of light that brings the veins to the surface of the skin."

As Izzy speaks, the visitor compares the room in which he sits to the words inside his head.

"The desks made me sad. The particleboard, the wood-grained Arborite, the crimped steel tubes, pieced together with no regard for structural logic. Was this my library?"

The man with the high shoulders does not look at the visitor. They are both silent.

"In the most important sense it was not. My library was a vast cube of water, through which Mr. Arrensen and I swam, taking heed of sharks and urchins and gradually gathering barnacles with the aim of attaining the wisdom of shipwrecks. The light was the barely filtered brilliance of a tropical noon: it penetrated the surface in shafts, which diminished below us to mere hints at a secret ocean floor. Most of the sun was trapped in the surface above us, so that it presented a ceiling of light whenever we looked up from our books, a ceiling beyond which the brightness was unimaginable. That was how the library was at that time.

"But I was impressionable, and perhaps I exaggerated the atmosphere in my bewitched mind, encouraged by subtle experiences. I know, for instance, that when I looked at Mr. Arrensen for the first time, his gray skin flashed silver and reflected the light prismatically. And sometimes, when he believed he was not being watched, he would open his mouth in a hinged manner uncharacteristic of our species, and his eyes would grow large and milky.

194

"I allowed him to introduce me to stories. Each book contained a world, and that I could keep so many worlds inside my head at once was for me a constant source of wonder: I felt as if I were every day entering a new room, which then expanded to fill my whole world, without displacing that world in any way. It did not make sense.

"Only later would I discover how radically my world had in fact been displaced."

Simonides closed his eyes and felt the wind rush through his deadened skull. There, on the first two seats, were the twin tax collectors from Thebes. He could not remember their names, but the first had a bladder purse hanging from a drawstring around his neck, and from this fact the widows could discern between them. On the third seat, the goldsmith from Rhodes, on the fourth . . . And so on, around the table.

Simonides found that he could conjure a mental picture almost as vivid as true sight. When speaking, he always met the eyes of his audience; one by one, he would look deep into each staring face, and for a moment each listener would become his personal interlocutor. In this way his speeches had the intimacy of conversation; each individual felt almost as if he were alone in a quiet room with the poet, receiving his full attention.

Because he had stared into each face many times over, he could recall each of the banqueters from the position of the chairs in which they had been crushed.

From this feat, which became instantly famous (grateful

widows being the way they are), Simonides derived the first thesis concerning the artificial memory: the architectural model, which became central to the theory of rhetoric in the Greek and Roman worlds. It survived the Middle Ages in the works of Cicero and Quintilian, but its fullest description comes to us in an arid handbook of rhetoric, falsely attributed to Cicero (and hence preserved with reverence in the monasteries): the mysterious *Ad Herennium.*

I have an urge to turn to this man sitting beside me, this gray man whose shoulders point towards the ceiling like the wings of a bat, and ask him: Do you know of a woman named Katie?

When I turn to him, however, he is gone. I am sitting alone in a library, surrounded by tiny desks and chairs. The wind is loud against the windows.

An orator would be required to eulogize the dead. Simonides was the natural choice. Seventy-four widows came to his house, each beseeching him to sing the praises of her crushed mate.

The fashion was for lengthy, detailed praise. Simonides would have to learn every positive feature even dubiously attributed to the dear departed. It was decreed that all of the bodies would be buried, sequentially according to rank, in a single lavish funeral. The orations would be delivered end to end. For the first time in his life, Simonides decided that it would be best to prepare.

The placement of the bodies around the table had

196

prompted his memory in a surprisingly efficient manner, and he thought to use a similar technique to recall the myriad details of his speech

He began by memorizing a sequence of rooms: the chambers of his own house. Beginning with the bedroom, Simonides mentally placed a piece of his speech in each chamber. He then closed his eyes and strolled through the rooms in his mind, casually picking up pieces of his subject matter as he went, and found that he could easily recall every detail.

The opening remarks, generalized comments about the horror of imperfectly constructed roofs, and a lament for the untimely crushed, were placed in the bedroom: he remembered this portion by imagining a large crack in the bedroom ceiling and a nasty bloodstain on the carpet below. He then walked into the mental hall, where he found the next portion of his speech sitting on a chair outside the bedroom door: the porcine host, impaled on a fork. Amusing himself greatly, Simonides attached the host's praiseworthy attributes (mostly spurious) to the various bathroom utensils. In this way he furnished his mental house with the necessary facts to be remembered.

Seventy-four crushed men. His own house did not have enough rooms to memorize the details pertaining to even one of these. He found himself walking, mentally, out into the street, and into his neighbor's house, and then into the house next door to that. To recall the entire speech, Simonides was forced to build, in his mind, the entire city.

The funeral orations lasted seven days and seven

nights. Simonides hired a slave to sit by the podium: Whenever he began to nod off, the slave would poke him in the ankle. The widows fell gratefully to sleep, one by one, after hearing the praises of their own dead husbands, only to be awakened by the keening of the next mourner. Simonides spoke with consistency, feeling, and beauty. He spoke for an entire week without intermission. In the course of his legendary speech, he mentally visited every room in every house of his grand and mournful city.

Dame Frances Yates, a scholar in the twentieth century, spent years researching the art of memory, and was amazed to discover that nobody had ever improved upon Simonides' technique.

"Mr. Arrensen," says the secretary in the principal's office, "retired seven years ago."

The man ponders this. He leaves the office and walks slowly to the front door. The boy is standing in the gutter by the side of the road, still bleeding.

Did you see the library?

Yes, I did.

Well?

The man does not answer. For some time, he follows the boy in silence.

I do not know how to speak about it, but I felt something pull at me as I sat there in the library. It pulled at me from another part of myself, the way the sound of an alarm clock tugs at the substance of a dream. I

198

did not properly awaken, however, and whatever it was that pulled at me has gone under again.

Places. Can they really call up forgotten worlds?

The young boy turns to me, as if he has heard the question inside my head.

Yes, he says. They can. When I first learned to speak, I used to walk through the city, in a big circle, and every place I saw put a new piece of the story in my head. The story was there, in the place, and all I had to do was walk through.

Nobody was ever there. Nobody listened to me. But I used to put on a tie anyway, because it seemed like something serious.

I used to take notes, said the boy. In case the story was forgotten.

Where are you taking me now?

To the stairwell.

When she met me, the doctors had given me little hope. I would never recover my episodic memory. Though I would remember how to do things, how to speak, write, drive a car, I would never remember the details of my life up to the point of the trauma.

It is assumed to be trauma, though I remember nothing. Once I cried out in my sleep, and though the doctors refuse to tell me what I said, they are convinced it is evidence of this: I underwent something, perhaps did something, which left me with an emotional burden too great for the conscious mind to bear. Under such cir-

cumstances, they say, the mind will often sabotage itself. In an effort to relieve the pain, it is not unusual
for the mind to erase great sections of the episodic
memory. The memory of events.

In most cases, the erasure is contained. A few weeks
or months are lost. The most unbearable stretch of
memory is erased, but the rest remains intact.

For some reason, however, I have lost everything.

The doctors have put forward two possible explana-
tions. The first theory, less probable, suggests that my
entire life to the point of amnesia was one cumulative
trauma; that I therefore had to erase the full sweep of
my past in order to make consciousness bearable. The
second theory, widely supported, suggests that I experienced a single trauma so potent that the mind has
overcompensated in its attempts to rid itself of the burden; in a spasm of self-disgust, it has erased far more
than was necessary.

Whatever the cause, all of the doctors agree that it
would be best not to attempt to retrieve the past. I
have been told to avoid psychoanalysis and hypnosis;
though both are sometimes capable of restoring the
memory after a traumatic event, they are thought dangerous. The trauma must have been sufficient to war-
rant the mind's reaction; I may have been lucky, in fact,
to have experienced nothing more than global amnesia.
The alternatives, often witnessed, are considerably worse.
A crippling of the will. Severe and incurable depres-
sion. Madness.

It has been two years, during which I have developed a new life. I have two years' worth of history now,

dominated, I must confess, by the hungry attentions of the woman I was lately to marry. I have had a hard time becoming close to people, though I consider myself affable, because the question of my erased history makes me seem somehow suspect: either a liar, or mentally ill. She, however, has always been strangely intrigued by my predicament: "I can have all of you," she once said with a wet smile, a look that pulled at me the way these leaves cling to my feet in death.

As the leaves fall about me, I think about Izzy. Every movement of the air sends more of these violent colors to the pavement. Why did he come now, this shivering creature with his crime? Why did he choose me for his confessor? I have had my own troubles—more than most—and with this marriage I would at last have become a citizen of this place, a respected citizen. I don't need doubts, not now, when it is important to be resolute.

I do not see ghosts; I am a thoroughly modern man. I find these stories of his fantastical—lies, essentially—contemptible and silly. So much of it has to be a lie. And I wonder if Katie exists.

Still silent, I follow the boy with the bleeding forehead through the streets of the city.

A young girl is sitting there, in the base of the stairwell, in yellow cashmere, alone. She draws on a cigarette, and her eyebrows pull together in worry.

I stand on the landing above, with the boy beside me.

We watch her for some time.

"What Margaret sensed in me," says Izzy, "what drove her to despair, was that I would never be able to love. She did not understand this in the abstract sense, however. We never do. All she knew was that I would never be able to love *her*.

"She was convinced, therefore, that the failing was hers, that she was in some fundamental way incapable of being loved.

"I did not mean her any harm. I was simply . . . preoccupied, and I had forgotten who she was. That she meant something. That I should treat her well.

"This very old story, you see, had found its way into my life.

"The story is one of abdication. A man, not necessarily a king, forgets what it is he is supposed to be, and incidentally causes great suffering. He loves a woman; she is never the protagonist; he briefly forgets what she is supposed to be, and incidentally destroys her.

"Something about this story makes it want to replicate, breed inwardly like cancer. Plays within plays, stories within stories: the smallest part of this tale contains within it, like a hologram, the beginning, middle, and end.

"I have told you, already, what this story is going to be."

Yes, he was told, but in the confusion of the moment, he has forgotten almost everything. He stands, alone on the landing now—the young boy has disappeared—and tries to recall the story.

Whose story was it? Why did he not write it down?

Joshua took notes. I wonder where they are.

The girl in the yellow sweater grinds her cigarette out against her shoe. She opens the steel door and goes out into the schoolyard.

The man follows, thinking: Margaret?

She enters the front door of a hospital on University. A few minutes later, a light comes on in a window on the ninth floor.

I wonder if that was once Katie's room. I feel somehow certain that it was. So. Margaret knows about this room.

The light comes on, and the room, though far away, nine stories up, tears something out of my submerged intelligence, calls a ghost out of the buried night.

I wonder if in the long time that I have forgotten about Margaret she has not forgotten about me. Perhaps she could never quite shake her yearning for death; perhaps suicide has become an addiction in the wake of my love. I can see her in hospitals, singing songs of need, picking the flowers of need and addiction, tracing lines across her thin wrists.

I can see this, and I can see her shape floating against the light of that window. The light shines through her, making a lamp of her bones. Ghosts. And I shiver. *Ghosts*.

I sit for a long time on the darkened bench, staring up at the lit window, her soul hanging there.

A man comes out of the front door, his head bowed. I do not take much notice of him at first, but he sits on a bench next to me and begins a conversation.

"I don't agree," he said, "with the concept of visiting hours. Nothing heals like companionship, and if they exclude you from the hospital at a crucial time, it can be disastrous for the patient."

I look at him through the dark. His shoulders fold up against his neck like the folded wings of a bat. He looks old, though, much older than the man who sat beside me this afternoon in the library.

He does not know who I am, but then I have changed.

I know, however. It came to me, a moment ago, in the opening of that light on the ninth floor.

I know who I am.

"Mr. Arrensen."

He squints, trying to see me better in the shadows, but there is more than a space of darkness separating us. "I'm sorry. I don't recognize you."

"Izzy," I say. "Izzy Darlow." Because that is my name.

There is a moment of recognition. A man stares at a map of the city—his city—but for the longest time he cannot orient himself to the lines on the page. What does that arrow mean? Where do these crossed lines lie in real space? Is this color significant? And, the most important question: where is he in this picture?

Then, in a moment of synthesis, something becomes clear. The map suddenly says something. The lines cohere. They do not simply refer, they speak: *You have found your place.* The map reaches out to the city around you, and there is a moment of clarity, correspondence, reciprocity. The world pictures itself. The map becomes a mirror. Your face, reflected in the mirror, finds its ground in the cradling city.

"I used to be a student . . ."

"Isaiah."

There is a long silence, and then he stands and extends his hand. I shake it. My hands now shake, nerve-shot. He sits again beside me.

"What are you reading now?"

"Maps. Maps of the city. Plans. I'm becoming interested in memory."

"Are you."

It is like this when the locus yields its topic; when the room offers up its memory. There is a moment of integration, of clarity, of mapping onto. You place a memory in this room, and then, years later, you walk through, and in a brief synaptic flash the memory is again yours.

I am Izzy Darlow, comes the thought. I have sat upon this bench before. I have been here many times, waiting for that light to appear in the window on the ninth floor. Katie's light; the light of recognition; the light that takes that room and instantly shoots it through with a piece of my story.

"And how are you, Israel?"

"Not so well. You know . . ."

He smiles sadly, and shakes his head. "No, I don't know. No, Isaiah, I don't know how it is with you. The truth is, I never understood you."

I have nothing to say to this. Mr. Arrensen sits beside me, quietly, staring up at the hospital. He thinks for a long time before he speaks.

"But then, why should I? Why should I expect to understand you? Youth is complex, no less complex than any other age. I am an old man. Does that make me any better able to see into the soul of a boy who is merely the age of Keats, Rimbaud, who is already older than Chatterton? Hofmannsthal wrote his best verse when he was much younger than you are."

"I'm not a poet."

"That's not the point. I'm simply trying to demonstrate that youth is also mysterious. I have no right to pretend that I know you."

Our conversation is stiff and uncomfortable, as we try to feel out how the years have changed us. I, too, have much to assimilate: I have just come awake, fully awake, and my life is flooding through me like an evil tide. I am holding the story I was told in my office; I am holding it up against my self like a mirror.

What I was told in the school was true: Mr. Arrensen is no longer a librarian. He has retired, and now lives on a small farm near Kitchener. A good friend of his is dying in the hospital, and he has moved into town for a month to be closer.

"You always showed some promise, Isaiah. Even when you made me nervous, you never ceased to show promise. It sounds as if you haven't had an easy time of it."

No. No, as I now discover, I haven't.

"But it's never entirely too late."

Really? Did he think so?

"Oh yes, I think so." He nods, as if to reassure himself as well. "There's always something. You are going to have to live with what you've done—that's a given. What's done is set into the landscape like the ruins of a building. I suppose you can try to forget, but memory will out. The ruin is peopled with ghosts."

In a moment full of sickness, the boy with the bleeding forehead comes to mind. Joshua. The lisp is gone.

I am staring up at the window, through a film of salt. Mr. Arrensen can see that I am in some pain; he puts a hand on my shoulder.

"But there's always something to be done. You can't forget, perhaps, but you can remember. And you can take your memory with you."

He pauses.

"Perhaps you were not meant to build. Perhaps you were meant to wander."

I look up at Katie's window, and it seems to me that the moon is caught in the glass.

"You're never going to be innocent, Isaac."

He too looks up at that window, and I wonder what he sees.

I think I made him sad. He had hopes for me, and at best he can now hope that I will not be destroyed. This, I suppose, is how parents have to modify their expectations when their children prove weak, or foolish, or mean. They can hope that the child will escape a life of petty crime and imprisonment. But he is not going to be a leader of men.

I have taken the name Izzy now, and it sits well. Izzy. I cannot remember his story, at least not as mine. I remember him telling me, of course, but I cannot call up the experiences as my own. These are not the experiences that matter anyway. What I want to know are those other memories, the ones even Izzy could not recall: what he had done in the guise of another creature, a nocturnal creature with golden eyes. I want to know what kind of crime I have committed.

Simonides discovered that memory grows out of the ruins of a fallen house.

Centuries later, Rodin will sculpt the figure of a caryatid who falls beneath the stone she is made to support. For Rodin, she briefly comes alive and then dies like the spark of a synapse. He catches the moment in bronze: the precise moment at which an architectural ruin becomes memory.

Later still, the philosopher Bachelard will ask: "How can secret rooms, rooms that have disappeared, become abodes for an unforgettable past?"

Knowing none of this, the man decides to return to the fallen house of his childhood.

It is still there, broken on its lot.

Here is the scar on the front lawn where the elm used to be. And here is the scar—that's all it really is— where I used to live. Burnt timber, crushed brick, the roof and floor so close that there is hardly anything you could still call a room. The house has become a plan, a horizontal picture of itself, a pond that holds a reflection though they have taken the world away.

Even Josh's room has at last collapsed. I sit on a piece of the concrete foundation, stained with decay, and stare about me into bricks that used to be walls, into the walls that used to support taped sheets of paper, into sheets that once told the story of my life in so many voices that I felt it could not possibly be one man's narrative.

And the walls grow up around me for a moment, so that I feel myself caught in the structure, walled into the ghostly building as if it were my grave. And I hear a voice.

The singing is distant at first, muted as if it comes through solid walls, but slowly the house about me grows again transparent, then fades to ruin, and the voice becomes increasingly strong as it passes through less and less substance. It is all very dangerous, this attempt to people ruined space with old associations: ghosts, ghosts, Campbell and the generations of dead children, mischief and caprice.

White, still carrying livid marks from the bruising metal, his body scarred horribly from the falling car but his voice intact, a young boy walks across the path of my staring eyes, singing: his forehead is bleeding.

We say nothing, but I follow him as he walks. The city gathers about me, almost whole, and my poor battered brother, dead but still singing with the conviction of the living, leads me out and across the night.

Even at night, the city preserves itself in its own mind. It is smug, self-contained; it sees itself in the pale light of its own wealth and safety. This is all a matter of appearances, but even at night the city appears to itself in a way that denies all questions. Josh, however, is singing.

What he sings makes the city uneasy. The careful sense of itself that the city has nourished over years of peace and slow government is gradually called into question. Josh sings to the foundations.

The story he sings is one of memory. As we pass through Chinatown, he sings a story of a railroad, and of men severed by an ocean from their language. He sings about men sitting listlessly on the front steps of houses, severed by an ocean from their wives, who were forced to remain behind for fear that they should multiply and drown the emergent country in yellow blood.

Some of the shops and restaurants are Vietnamese, and here the foundations speak as we walk by. They murmur briefly with the fear long since forced from memory. The buildings above them creak with the sound of masts bending and ropes burning against the flesh. We pass and they settle again into silence.

Through the Jewish, Portuguese, Italian, and Brazilian quarters, now brightly identified with official signs so that tourists will know what kind of food they are eating; everything forgotten comes briefly and terribly to life. The city becomes its forgotten self, and the entire enterprise threatens to collapse into the blood of its foundations. We pass a man asleep in the shards of his bottle, whose eyes open for a moment when Josh sings the story of the land beneath the pavement. The man remembers the songs about his great-great-grandfather, who traded that land away for an empty bottle, now broken.

Josh sings, and the ruins beneath the foundations reveal their dead. He sings of what had to be forgotten to allow the city its growth; centuries of narrative emptied of blood, empires reduced to signs on the street and exotic cuisine.

And in the color of his song is a mute warning: you were homeless before, and you will be homeless again. Nothing this safe, nothing like this—expensive and banal—can ever be your eternal home. Count what you own, count it twice, examine your children asleep in their beds. You will take none of this into exile with you; your children will be slaves in another man's house and language.

We walk until morning. I have heard, for the first time, the silence of the city. I have seen everything, touched every stone twice, run my hand over every surface, emblazoned the map upon my soul.

When the sun is on the point of rising, an emerging glow beneath the yellow haze of the suburbs, Josh begins to lose stamina. He stumbles, and his voice breaks. For a moment he does not sing, but speaks incomprehensible words—Hebrew, I think—and his lisp returns.

"Where are you taking me? Josh, please don't disappear . . ."

But the morning breaks over the city, and that is precisely what he does. The bulbous sun pushes up, somehow not circular, pressed into a flowing ellipse by the weight of its rising, and with the flow of autumn light across the pavement he disappears.

Don't disappear.

Josh, don't disappear.

Who will tell the story?

The man stands on a broken square of sidewalk. On one side is the road. On the other, the land falls away and becomes wild. He stands with one shoulder to the city, and the other towards the ravine. Josh, whose circle always takes him home, the long way round, has left him here. The man walks to the edge of the ravine. Here the trees begin. He stares into the shadows.

The sun is well above the horizon now, and the shadows stretch across the city like bankers' fingers. In the ravine the sun has still to rise—it may never rise—and the entire wild space is dark.

What does he feel now, with the memory of the city still quick in him like a cut in the flesh? With his brother gone, lost a second time, though he had forgotten the first? Is he in mourning, or something worse? What kind of sickness comes with memory?

He does not yet feel whole. He has not yet come home. He now remembers what much of the city has forgotten: the song of violence at the city's founding. That is something. It places him in the landscape. But it is still abstract.

There is something more. I did something, which I have forgotten. I did something to myself, so that my past was torn from me. Trauma, the doctors say. What was this trauma?

212

Sick, but not yet at home, he steps carefully into the shadow, forgets the morning, and enters the ravine.

The disorder is immediate. Everything crawls over everything else in an effort to achieve the sun, and everything twists in its failure to do so, taking on the shape of disappointment. The city is ruled by the most simple mathematic, whereas the ravine grows into the shape of will, blind to reason, the form expressed by the original chaos. There is nothing of the garden here. It is not at all like a garden.

He has not eaten in some days. When his fiancée's father removed him from his position at the Archive, he had some money saved, enough to stay alive for a couple of weeks. It has been longer than that. He feels the constant presence of his stomach inside him: not memory this time, but hunger. In this way, he is now like every other creature in the ravine.

The shadows deepen as he descends. They deepen the way a room grows dark over decades, when trees grow between the window and the sun. There is a sense of time passing as he goes deeper. By the time he has reached the tangled space at the bottom, years have passed.

The time does not go in one direction only. It goes forward, slowly, and backwards, sometimes in great leaps. The space calls up memories. It calls up voices. He can hear the voices around him.

Katie. I cannot seem to call up an image of her, but I now remember the scent of her hair. She seemed always to have a fever, Katie: her hair was always damp, and gave off the scent of damp hair.

Campbell. Why Campbell? Because he never went away. He disappeared, but he never went away. I have been haunted, since, and that is Campbell's doing. That is his place in my life. He is the one who haunts me.

Aaron. My father. My mother. Sapphire.

There are voices in the space around me. If I close my eyes, I become sick with memory. It is like being in Josh's room, with those stories everywhere, in every dimension, in the shape of the city.

Katie: Do you like to look at me, Izzy? Am I still good to look at?

Izzy: I can't see you . . .

Campbell: I have found something tremendously valuable.

Izzy: What, Campbell?

Campbell: Something we want.

Aaron: It can be done . . .

Father: You cannot be loved.

Mother: The boy will suffer.

The placement of voices in space is drama.

He spends seven nights in the ravine, and the moon grows from a small hard sliver, the clipping from a fingernail, to a bowl of milk, white and round in the black field of the sky.

He has become thirsty.

The voices will not quit. He hears them in the hollow of the tree, where the branch has rotted out; he hears them in the damp space between the stone and the soil; he hears them in his head.

Professor Gold: What you call memory is simply this: images in fading sepia of—what?—women you have groped instinctively; perhaps men you have lain down before out of boredom or the need to be punished . . .

Margaret: You only like to hear me breathe like this because you think it's you who makes my breath sound this way . . .

Margaret, thinks Izzy: Margaret.

And with the certainty of memory he knows this: Margaret is dead.

It is another moment of recognition, but this one brings terror. How dangerous is this memory? Were these the words that he called out once in his sleep? The trauma? Was it Margaret's death that placed him here, in pieces and voices at the bottom of the ravine?

There had been a phone call at midnight. He did not yet work at the Archive; his memory was still intact. (What will remembering do? Am I going to lose the story again?) He had long since left Katie.

He remembers the room he lived in at that time. A tiny room across the bridge, off the Danforth in the Greek district. There was the succession of small jobs that had kept him alive. And his family. He had fallen out of touch with his family; as far as he knew, only Aaron and his father remained in contact. His father was still in real estate, although he was running for alderman. Aaron made machines for hospitals; he had developed a special interest in psychosurgical technology.

His mother was wandering. The last he heard, she was visiting relatives in Ethiopia. Did they have relatives in Ethiopia?

He had no friends, and the phone almost never rang. At midnight, however, on this night of the full moon, he was woken by the sound of the telephone beside his bed.

The telephone, with its yellowing dial, was made of that heavy black plastic that has since disappeared. The bell was mechanical, loud and palpable, the sound of an emergency, an angry acoustical ring.

"Izzy? Am I speaking to Izzy Darlow?"

"Yes."

"Ah." The woman paused, as if to gather strength. The voice was diminished, but not weak. "Ah. Then I've found you."

"Margaret?"

"I'm dying, Izzy. Tonight. It's a good night to die. Have you seen the moon?"

Her voice, though weak, was not strained. She spoke of her death as a fact, a pleasant occurrence of some importance, but nothing frightening or pitiful.

"Yes . . ." I could see the moon through my window, low and orange, with a perfect circular edge. "Yes, I can see it. How are you, Margaret?"

"That seems like a silly question. It seems foolish to ask that question of a woman who is going to be dead within the hour. But I'm glad you ask, Izzy. I'm fine. I've never been better. How are you?"

216

"I'm not well, Margaret."

"No. No, I guess you're not."

I did not know what to say. Margaret waited, breathing lightly.

"I'm . . ."

"What are you, Izzy? I'd really like to know."

"I'm . . . sorry."

"You're sorry."

She paused again. When she spoke, her voice was fainter, as if it were on its way out.

"I only phoned you, Izzy, to say—"

She was silent.

"To say what, Margaret?"

"To say . . . that you might want to look into it. The mystery of who you are. You're not an easy person to love, Izzy. It's hard to love you. It's painful to try. It's . . . destructive. You might want to look into that."

The silence, now, was mine.

"I'm dying, Izzy."

"Where am I going to look, Margaret?"

"I don't know. Surely there's someone out there who can remind you of who you are, of what you do to people, of what you've done . . ."

"Margaret?" Then louder: "Margaret?"

The line did not go dead, yet there was no one at the other end.

I thought about Margaret's last request. And I remembered a boy who had done precisely this, once, who had made me think on who I was and what I'd done, a boy who had marked my life with his leaving that first time I moved Margaret to consider suicide.

I found myself standing at the place in the center of the road where the manhole had appeared, first to Joshua and then to Campbell, on those nights long ago. The moon was full. There was a shape emerging in the blank surface of the pavement; the manhole was returning, and when it appeared it was open. The moonlight fell into the deep shaft at my feet.

Sick with anticipation, I began to crawl down the rungs of the ladder, feeling the rust against my hands. I levered myself down through the deep shaft, slowly—I shall always be terrified of falling—until my feet touched bottom.

There was an audience.

The abandoned subway station had been converted into a theater. There were risers on the platforms on either side of the sunken area through which the tracks ran. Over this chasm an ordinary ladder lay like a bridge. Lights were hung from a grid of plumbing; some were mounted on handles and carried by actors. I climbed onto a riser and took a seat; the performance was about to begin.

Someone passed me a program. The play was called *Ophelia,* by William Shakespeare. At the center of the stage, always, was a woman with a noose around her neck. The rope was slack and tied to the ceiling. It effectively drew an invisible circle within which she could move without choking. Mostly she was consigned to the ladder that lay across the center of that circle, but there was also some space on the platforms to either side where she was free to move about.

She had a lover named Hamlet with whom she would banter. Sometimes she would forget the noose, and move in a way that almost throttled her. At these times she would return to the center of the stage. She would walk across the ladder, carefully, and stand in the center. Then she would take a stone from her pocket and drop it into the pit below. There would be a splash; a deep pit had been dug between the tracks and flooded with water.

There was a character called the Player, who was hooded like a hangman. At the very beginning of the play, Hamlet instructed the Player in his craft: how the play ought to be structured and performed in order to catch the conscience of the King.

At a certain moment, paper crowns were placed on the heads of the audience. They were each given a paper cup full of liquid and told not to drink because it was poison.

The woman seemed very much in love with her lover, but he had something on his mind. Though he was not specifically bent on doing her wrong, he was concerned with something—something that had nothing to do with her. It made him behave in peculiar ways. Everything he did, in fact, caused the rope to burn against her neck, prevented her from breathing, sent her over the tracks to drop a stone into the water below.

The words were from Shakespeare, but they had been rearranged. Some were repeated in litanies; some were fragmented into nonsense. The import, however, was unmistakable. A man was obsessed. A woman, who had committed no crime except that she loved too much, was going to be destroyed.

The Player was joyful. He was responsible for the action. He instructed the actors carrying lights to illuminate certain scenes. He moved objects about the stage. He never said a word, but he danced with high steps, and you knew that he was smiling beneath his hood.

At a crucial moment, when the woman was no longer capable of making real sense, when she was reduced to dragging a steel chain laced with flowers across the floor, the Player walked into the audience and took me by the hand. He led me out onto the stage, wordlessly, and I took part in the play. For a while, I was thrilled to be on stage.

He instructed me, without speaking, to remove the ladder from the pit. I pulled it across towards me, and placed it over my shoulders. The Player had me stand to the side, with the ladder over my shoulders, to watch the end of the play.

Ophelia was dragging her chain about the stage, singing, and Hamlet was off in a corner, speaking a soliloquy into a wall. At one point she saw him, and reached out towards him, and cried out, but the noose tightened on her neck and she almost choked.

As always, she walked back to the center of the stage. Now, however, there was no ladder across the tracks, and when she stepped off the edge into the air she fell into the water, making a sound like a stone. The noose tightened and the rope went taut. Her eyes opened. Her body shivered. She swung from side to side, and the noises that she made were not singing.

Hamlet, her lover, turned away from the wall. He ran over to the tracks, to be with Ophelia, but as he jumped he too fell and had to hold on to her swinging body to keep from plunging headlong into the water. As his weight clung to hers she made a last noise and stopped shivering and became still.

Hamlet stole the words from Laertes' mouth, and cursed himself:

Oh! treble woe
Fall ten times treble on that cursed head,
Whose wicked deed thy most ingenious sense
Depriv'd thee of!

The houselights went up, and I remained standing over to the side, with a ladder about my neck. The Player stood next to me, as he took his bow, and with a flourish he removed his hangman's hood.

There had been clues in the movement of his small body throughout the play, a joyful delinquency I had found familiar. Also, I remembered suddenly, I had come here for a reason. But I had been too caught up in the play, in the obsessions that had destroyed this poor woman, incidentally, though she had done nothing wrong, to think much on what lay beneath the black mask. Thus, when he showed his face and bowed to the audience as I carried the bridge on my shoulders, I was as surprised as I might have been had I never suspected.

The Player was Campbell.

I stood for hours with the ladder cutting into my shoulders, until the stage emptied, and then the house. Campbell disappeared, but I had found what I was looking for; I had no desire to follow him. The empty noose swung over the hole in the center of the tracks.

Ophelia returned, naked, carrying her costume. She did not seem to see Izzy, standing there.

"I'm a seagull," she muttered to herself. "No, that's wrong. Remember you shot a seagull? A man happened to come along, saw it and killed it, just to pass the time. A plot for a short story. No, that's wrong. What was I saying? I was talking about the stage . . ."

She fingered the empty noose, frowned, then wandered off.

He stands in the dark of the ravine, staring up at the lit window in the side of the house. Staring at the window, he remembers everything. Most of all, he remembers the precise moment when he chose to forget.

It was the play. The play that made everything so clear: what he had done, who he was. I came to you, Katie, three times with torn green pieces, and then a fourth. I lied to you, about how we met: we did not meet in the hospital, Katie.

I put you in the hospital.

There was a book, and a machine. I cut a part away from myself, and it visited you. The drama had made clear what I had done. It was an event, however, that I had not wanted to know. In the full light of memory, I had found my guilt unspeakable, unbearable; I had made myself forget.

It is not so easy, however. The truth will out, said Mr. Arrensen. The truth will out. Since that night, in the forgotten part of the earth beneath the city, when I made myself forget what Campbell had made me remember, since that night, I have had visitors of my own.

I have been forced to remember again. To meet with the self I cut away. It is no longer a mystery to me why Campbell was there in my life, why he did what he did. From the very start, he was fulfilling Margaret's last request: he was there to remind me of who I was.

It was not Campbell's fault that the memory was too strong and that I made myself forget. (I have spent hours trying to reach the house, the one with the lit window in the side, but it cannot be reached from this place in the ravine. So I have made my way back up to the road.) No, it was not Campbell's fault.

Over here, at the top of the road, by the side of the park and the reservoir, is a path I have walked up before, when the moon was bloated and full. Over here, where the pavement yields to crushed twigs, a path of kindling that winds through the edge of the wooded park, skirting the manmade lake, then descending into the dark ravine—over here is a path even Izzy did not remember, in telling me his story, because part of himself had been torn away to commit a crime. That part was me.

Aaron's machine, which had been designed to bring a wolf cub to life, had given life to something else. Machines often do. We design them for a purpose, but we cannot restrict them to that purpose. They are like us: increasingly voracious, infinite in potential desire, unbounded in the capacity to destroy.

Design a simple knife, and it will tell you two stories as it is passed from hand to hand: the story of surgery, and the story of torture. Aaron's machine—the first of many machines, and I wonder sometimes what his increasingly sophisticated machinery will accomplish—brought something to life, something perhaps canine, perhaps not, but certainly not at all what he had intended.

I descend on the path, and the house comes into sight. I remember this path, and I remember this house. As before, it is effortless to step up to the window, that window so tall that a man can enter without bending his head. I simply wish myself onto the window ledge. The curtains with their living patterns move like trees in the wind and I brush them aside with a careful hand. She is there.

The furniture has grown roots and branches as it has always threatened to do; the room is wrapped about with tendrils and leaves and vines; seeds from the Continent of Forgetting nurtured by poor mad Katie have grown into a forest here and the walls are obscured by creeping life. She is there.

I had forgotten how much she looks like who she is.

Curled into a corner like a knot in the root of the great tree that was once her bedpost, Katie stares up at me with starving eyes and neither fears me nor welcomes me nor knows me at all.

"Katie?"

She seems to have some sense that that is her name, that once she was called Katie, but she has been torn roughly from the earth that grounded her and now she knows nothing. She reaches out a hand to touch me as I approach.

I wondered what she might be when I saw her but I did not expect this: childlike, her sense crippled, her body still wrapped up in that thin hospital gown, but gone, gone, gone. I take her into my arms and it is like lifting an armful of leaves: she could come apart in my hands and drift about me in fading colors. I collect her in my arms and hold tight.

"Katie, do you remember who I am?"

She does not understand me, but touches my lips to see whether she can identify the source of this miracle: a human voice. I kiss her finger and she smiles, pulling it away.

I take her in my arms and hold tight, so that she will not come apart, so that she will not drift into pieces about my feet like the leaves in the ravine.

I have no doubt that I have made the right decision, the first real decision in years.

I will take Katie with me, and tell her this story. I will tell her the full story this time, of how we met: I will tell her those parts that Izzy did not remember.

I appeared, Katie, four times on the night of the full moon. I gave you three gifts and on the fourth night left you with nothing.

Some day she will understand words again, he thinks. Later still she will comprehend the story. Then she will judge him. The years ahead will be hard, and he hopes that she will acknowledge this: that she will see something in the way that he carries himself, that she will acknowledge his difficulty. He will tell her everything. He has a story to tell.

He hopes that she will take his story, and read penitence in the lines on his face. He hopes that she will not judge him too harshly.

He carries her in his arms like a gathering of leaves, holding tight so that she will not drift into pieces and settle about the floor, but a wind comes up from the ravine below. A wind comes up and carries through the broken windows, stirring the curtains. The scent of mildew fills the room. A wind comes up, and scatters the leaves in his arms so that they drift, for a moment, in the churning air of the room, and then settle into the roots of the floor.

She is not there.

She has not been there for some time. There is nothing there but the decay of a house, long since offered up to the whims of the ravine. A doll sits in the corner, smiling a half-smile.

It is too late, of course. Now that he has a story to

tell, there is no one there to listen. Is this the cost of remembering who he is?

Katie, where are you?

The room is silent, except for the wind that rises up and out of the ravine below. The leaves eddy. The twisted one smiles.

He strains to hear, but the room is silent.

He strains to hear.

Somewhere, perhaps only in his memory, he can hear a seagull crying.

ABOUT THE AUTHOR

Douglas Cooper was born in Toronto. After taking an M.A. in philosophy, he led safaris in Kenya, wrote feature screenplays for Talisman Films in London, and settled for a time in Paris, where he completed this novel. He now lives in New York.